ODDNÝ EIR

LAND OF LOVE AND RUINS

Translated by
Philip Roughton

RESTLESS BOOKS
BROOKLYN, NEW YORK

First published as *Jarðnæði* by Bjartur & Veröld, Reykjavík, 2011

First Restless Books paperback edition October 2016

ISBN: 9781632060723
Library of Congress Control Number: 2016940765

Cover design by Helen Yentus
Set in Garibaldi by Tetragon, London

Printed in the United States of America

1 3 5 7 9 8 6 4 2

Ellison, Stavans, and Hochstein LP
232 3rd Street, Suite A111
Brooklyn, NY 11215

www.restlessbooks.com
publisher@restlessbooks.com

This book has been translated with financial support from

Icelandic
LITERATURE
CENTER
MIÐSTÖÐ ÍSLENSKRA BÓKMENNTA

LAND OF LOVE AND RUINS

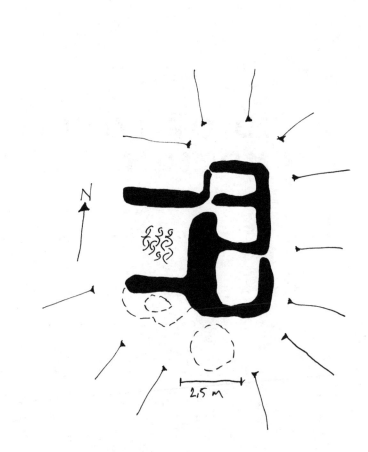

The illustrations on this page and page 230 are archaeological plans,
drawn by Uggi Ævarsson, of the ruins of farm sites at Hólsfjöll, northern Iceland

For ornithologists and archaeologists

He thought that it would be as sweet thus to lie so in the grave, to hear the peaceful sounds of the earth and just to know that one's dear friends were near.

DOROTHY WORDSWORTH
GRASMERE JOURNALS

Those were fun times in the attic.
I remember how we always plucked twenty or so ptarmigans.
We sang and told stories and laughed our heads off.
But it was most fun after we'd finished and cleaned everything up,
when, covered in feathers, we'd go out and roll around in the snow.

ODDNÝ ÓLAFSDÓTTIR
SEASONAL MEMORIES

I t's strange being home. I'm relieved, though I still feel a bit homesick. I've got to try to create a home of my own. Probably alone. Could maybe get a dog. Shame how much trouble it is to travel overseas with dogs. Are they put in the baggage compartment?

Love is blind, and it's not the only one. I feel like I'm blindfolded. I'm going to untie the blindfold, write on it in the gleam of dawn. The sun is being reborn.

M om and I went for a drive this afternoon, took a look at houses.

Drove past one that she said was probably good for nurturing your spirit. It reminded me of the countless drives in and around the city in search of a house when we felt it was getting too crowded in our own, which Mom called a dirt hut at bad moments. Then we went home, where my dad and brother were hanging up ptarmigans. It might not be under the best of circumstances, but we'll spend Christmas together, the old family, my brother and I both in our late thirties and newly single, seeking refuge in our childhood nest. Nowadays, it's quite festive when the four of us get together, despite our various wounds, or maybe because of them. It gives me grounding, strength.

A tree that's been struck by lightning but still has its needles. Poisonous red berries can be made medicinal if they're handled properly and distilled.

He came up to the attic last night, wearing black, tightly woven woolen clothes, fragrant with green cologne. I caught a whiff of his sweet sweat, and sensed straightaway that his ballsack had blossomed. The ornithologist whom I met at the clinic last year has come to town, even more beautiful than when I saw him when he was ill; now he simply shines.

Do you live here? His clear, blue eyes awaited a reply. No, this is my workspace, I said, finding it funny that he thought I lived in such a cubbyhole. He glanced around, and I got the feeling it was to see if we could make love in this lair. The place was far from soundproof, I pointed out, and surrounded by scholars trying to concentrate. I offered him a seat on my little cot. I asked him where he lived and he described a small basement apartment: right nearby, beautiful patterns in the cement, he said, but full of ghosts, even rats; he wanted to find another place as soon as possible, was in a kind of limbo.

I lent him a walkie-talkie; the channel is open so we have to develop our own code. Before he left, he took an ivy leaf from a book that was in his pocket and handed it to me, with greetings from Pentagonia, the kingdom of dark green pentangles. Should we get ourselves a place there? I said of course.

He left just before midnight. I wanted to keep working for a while and challenge my fear of the dark to a duel. But he called me on the walkie-talkie as soon as he got home and I ran over to his place and stayed until morning. I didn't smell any rats, but had bad dreams. You can't enter another person's world too quickly; you've got to sift through. I've often set out rather carelessly, say no more, *over and out*.

When I saw him, I found him so grown-up and mature that I imagined he'd cleaned out all his old junk and rubbish. Disappointing to discover the infantile fluff still in his navel. But you never fully cleanse yourself of primordial shame and dirt. As soon as your heart opens, its waste pours out along with the love. But then it's a good idea to keep pumping and pumping, replace your septic tanks and your connection with the sea, so that you can enjoy peace and quiet in your own house, your own privy place.

Privy is certainly a peculiar word. Where's my etymological dictionary? Is it a corruption? "A privy place to rest and think," like a chapel, quiet and peaceful, perfect for contemplation—can chapels and toilets have so much in common? Is it a place where a real connection is made between the lowest chakra, the anus, and the highest, the divinity in our head? Or is it a place of quietude for the watchful eye of high heaven, just as you ground your waste in a radical transformation? In the homes of the European aristocracy, the most fruitful conversations of the day took place in the privy, as the householders were expelling yesterday's excess in preparation for the new day. There in the privy, they tidied themselves, spritzed on the newest perfumes in the province, and expounded their latest theories.

I'm finishing writing up the memoirs of my grandmother, my namesake, and rhymes and verses from her childhood. I'm going to print them out and bring them to her today—it's her birthday and she'll be serving crepes with whipped cream, maybe even bring out her pink tableware. Her memoirs begin on Epiphany, when it was customary to make crepes, as was also customary when a child was born—the maid must have been so glad to get out of baking for one day when Grandma was born.

Then there are the rhymes that she recites with such a rollicking lilt that putting them on paper does them little justice:

To the Alþing they came
a carl and beldame
returned with a bird
in a mitten, I've heard
And when they came home
they were given a bone
cracked by a stone
The man then spoke up:
"It's time that we sup!"
and in came a dish
bearing wet fish
a trout fine to eat
and four grilled pig's feet
The carl took his pick
grabbed a foot quick
and a man it became

Grettir by name
This Grettir is skilled in many a thing
crossed the deep, put maidens to sleep
cows and calves and even the king

S trolled around the lavafield this morning, found a secluded spot amid the bearberry bushes and pumice. I felt exposed when a ptarmigan flew over as I was squatting there; it came so close to the crown of my head, circling and croaking. I feel a bit tense, having just come from the commotion of the city and hardly knowing what anything means. Why again do they circle like that?

I went back to the tent and he was still sleeping, so I smacked him with a twig and howled *cream puff, cream puff!* He barely stirred, turned onto his other side. So I undressed and slipped into his down sleeping bag, clamped my thighs around his legs, sniffed his neck, and ran my hand over his warm scrotum.

We woke at the same time and told each other how badly we'd dreamed—unpleasant memories from old relationships. We could barely look at each other. Maybe a person's head clears faster near volcanoes. Hekla could erupt at any moment, but right now I fear so much more than its fire.

The unfilled cream puffs that I brought with me have all been squashed to pieces beneath the jam jar.

We took a long walk through the lava, saying nothing at first. It feels comfortable keeping silent, even though it's strange to walk with someone you don't know very well without exchanging a single word. It took me time to trust the silence between us, to feel that it wasn't just a lack of connection. I tried to be independent and not think about how he felt or how our relationship really was, why we might be at odds. But when I forgot both myself and him and started looking down between my feet at the winter flowers here and there amid the traces of snow, some cocky fox kits yelped in a crevice, startling me so much that I lost my footing and plunked down onto the moss. I was terrified, remembering a story that my brother Owlie had just told me about a fox that attacked an archaeologist, clamping its sharp, savage teeth around her calf.

Laughing, he pulled me to my feet, and, with a furtive look, led me into a small, deep lava cave, covered with damp moss. I got the gist of his intentions, found a nice, soft spot, lay on my back and took him in my arms, and he found his way in through our woolen clothing. We moved in rhythm to the joyful sounds of a snow bunting, which lets itself be blown through the sky, unafraid of volcanic eruptions.

On the way back, he told me that his great-grandfather had bought this land and that he could build a cottage here if he wanted to, whenever he was able. Could you imagine living here with me for part of the year? he asked. Yes, I definitely thought I could. It's my dream to live close to the wilderness, in perfect peace and quiet. You don't need complete solitude, then? he asked. No, I don't think so, I said.

The winter wren's so swollen-headed that it's on the verge of bursting. I injected cream into the remains of the choux puffs and we chowed them down.

The stress seeps from you gradually. The city's soot. I've been writing lists of words that end in two "s's" in Icelandic: *fúss, rass, hoss, spíss, koss, fliss, kross, piss, fuss, suss, tráss, góss, hnoss, hress, bless* . . . I found forty words.

I have no idea how to go about creating a clues-in-squares crossword puzzle, but we decided to try it together. The answer should be one particular word, isn't that right? Or one sentence? I thought of the word *næði* (peace, quiet, privacy, leisure) or *náð* (rest, quiet, grace) or *jarðnæði* (piece of land, farm tenancy). He said it might be better to have the word *náðhús* (privy, restroom) or *náhús* (tomb), even *gröf* (ditch, grave), and added that there I would find perfect peace and quiet. We bickered a bit and I feel as if I still need to explain to him my dream of privacy. He headed down to the heath to check on a nest and try to find a path that he saw on an old map.

We were hit by something of a storm and took shelter in his great-grandfather's little house, which had previously been a workshed in Reykjavík. This great-grandpa was prescient, being a foreigner, and foresaw the value of the land, stipulating in his will that it couldn't be sold off from the family. We found a full gas cylinder and some excellent cider. With our first sip, this verse sprang into his mind:

> *Concealed by lava in our own secret lair*
> *to the depths of our souls sheer joy we share,*
> *may God, dearest darling, pay heed to my prayer*
> *that he grant you rich earth,*
> *quietude and mirth*

in a sun-blessed bower,
there to reflect on this blissful hour
of refuge, delight,
'neath Hekla's great height.

We're sitting at a cloth-covered oaken table; he's reading and I'm writing. I have to deliver a manuscript shortly, but still haven't found the right tone. He's excited to finish a book by Thomas Bernhard, about a man who has an entire novel in his head and is always waiting to find enough peace and quiet to start writing it. Does he succeed? No, the years pass, as his wife incessantly knits a wool mitten and unravels it as soon as she's finished, until finally her husband murders her.

W e decided to sleep in the cottage that evening, after the wind picked up quite a bit. Got our sleeping bags and laid them on the beds, where there were little down pillows embroidered with the words *Sleep tight*. He came to my bed and cuddled with me. We felt warm and fuzzy from the cider. Then he lay down again in his own bunk and began wondering aloud where he should build his hut in the future, our hut. He pointed out that there was no single spot that possessed all the land's virtues, and asked me to prioritize: Mt. Hekla in sight, shelter from the weather, sunshine from the south, a panoramic view, a ready water supply, peace and quiet. Then we heard a thud. He went out, bare-bottomed, with a flashlight, and returned with the news that the deck table had blown over, but everything was all right. I admired his courage: to wade naked into the darkness. In a short time, he fell asleep and started snoring manfully.

I couldn't relax; my nerves were taut and my mind raced. I thought I'd outgrown my fear of the dark. I tried to find a scientific explanation: the southerly had shifted to a northerly, as he said. I wondered if the traces of body odor mingled with perfume on the pillow would be enough to call old ghosts to mind. I'd assumed I would be welcome in this cute little house, yet I didn't feel at home here. Ever since I was little, homesickness has hit me like hail from a clear blue sky. I lay there stiffly for a long time, until the day began to dawn, when I dressed and went out to the tent, feeling like it was more my own. I wrapped myself in woolen shawls and sweaters from my grandmothers.

It isn't particularly easy to be a guest in other people's homes. On farms in the old days, hospitality was measured by how guests were made welcome in the home, whether invited or not—the latter including those who hadn't made plans ahead of time, as well as those who just dropped by in search of food and shelter.

It might be easy to be an invited guest, but to be uninvited and reliant on others must be hard for anyone.

I could imagine becoming a gypsy, if they weren't dependent on others so much of the time. If they were self-reliant and dancing free, as in my dreams.

I remember when I met a swarthy gypsy clan-leader and followed him into a big white tent on the outskirts of the forest. He warned that his extended family had been harassed and refused shelter so often that it had grown suspicious and less hospitable than it would have liked to be. And I didn't like the look of things inside the sweaty tent; it seemed their solidarity hinged on desperation, like at a family reunion in the remotest part of a fjord in bad weather. The instruments out of tune.

A woman wearing a beautiful headpiece offered to read my palm, which I accepted, reaching into my pockets for anything I had, and she said that I would be wandering a long time; it was as if there were a curse that would prevent me from finding a place to be for the time being. Her eyes filled with compassion and she said that I was clearly some kind of gypsy, a ruddy gypsy, but that I had to clear off—I didn't belong with them. Spoke to me like a dog, as the gypsies have so often been spoken to: *Get out of here, scram, go on, git!*

I must have dozed a bit; woke to find him attempting to zip our sleeping bags together, then giving up. The wind reverberates in the mountains and the storm whips the tent flap. Impossible to take a nap in this. What hellish currents are these? Would you rather be Eggert or Bjarni? he asked me with a laugh, just before he fell asleep. He told me that the explorers Eggert and Bjarni had in fact camped here the night before they hiked up Hekla and became the first people to discover that it isn't a gateway to Hell. I once dreamed about Bjarni in a lustful love-game with a loon on the wooden floor of his apothecary. And the only thing I know about Eggert is his *Georgic*, although I noticed the two men's travel journal in the box of books in the car.

I'm going to try to put myself to sleep by finding new "s"-words: *túss, skass, hlass, krass, hass, hoss, fliss, flass, trass, kross, gloss.* Did I already have *kross* and *fliss*? And *pluss*? What is *pluss*, anyway? Is it a genuine Icelandic word? I wish I'd brought my dictionary with me. Not that it's a perfect account of Icelandic. But it's a decent attempt. Those who put it together must have really needed peace and quiet.

Then there are the *mm*-words: *gúmm, skamm, djamm, gjamm, vamm, skömm* . . . and *búmm*, in honor of Bursting Day today.

Salted lamb and split-pea soup. I'm happy not to have to redo the dictionary, update it. It would drive me mad. Now I hear bleating. It certainly is nice that there are still sheep grazing and farmers sleeping soundly in their farmhouses amidst all the summer cottages. Few fear the old fox roving through the lava, russet and independent.

I went to visit Grandma around noon. Asked her what she thought of the summer cottages, whether she would have enjoyed staying in one over the years. She replied with an unequivocal *no*. She'd never felt comfortable in summer cottages; they weren't her style. Nor would she have wanted to live in the suburbs. Even if they're supposedly a nice place for children and dogs. She would rather shoot herself than have to walk a dog!

Once a week, a very charming man brings a gray dog to the retirement home and goes from room to room to allow the residents to pet it. She said that she told the man the dog was incredibly cute and probably fun, but that she didn't like dogs, and he hasn't come to her room since. Then came the story of the summer cottage.

Grandpa had just returned from a sea voyage. He reserved a little cottage. And good weather was predicted that summer. But he needed to spend more time in town than he'd thought, so Grandma was there alone with her three daughters and a very young babysitter.

By the end of summer, the girls had grown tired of the little home of their own that they'd created outside and were waiting to go and pick berries. They nagged their mother and asked:

When do the berries come, when is Daddy coming? They wanted him to pick berries with them and teach them about plants, as he usually did, about which ones could be used for dyeing and healing, and they wanted their mother to recite verses and teach them poems. That's the way it was supposed to be.

But by the time the berries were ripe, he came and made an announcement: that he was moving in with another woman. She needed him so much, and he her.

A few years later he came back to Grandma. They never rented a summer cottage again. Their home was beautiful, open to family and friends; a warm and welcoming country home in the center of town. Every day, visitors both invited or uninvited shared meals with them. At the dining table, issues were discussed; folk sat in rocking chairs late into the night. These weren't just men's clubs or sewing circles; the sexes were mingled and every generation was represented. There was singing and versifying, canned fruit cocktail eaten with whipped cream, or freshly picked blueberries from the north. On the weekends, drives were taken in the Cadillac through the city's outlying countryside to enjoy the view of the mountains, and everyone who wanted to join in, joined in.

I 'm sitting at my desk, looking at the sun. There's hardly any night these days, which means I'm not paralyzed by fear of the dark even though I'm alone in strange premises. I was invited to come and stay in a little apartment by the sea, which was previously used to store library books. It was as if my prayers had been answered, because I wanted so badly to get out of the city.

The man who came to fix the Internet connection told me that Kamilla, the librarian who smoked cigarillos on sunny days and played the accordion, had lived here for a long time. But you have nothing to fear, he said, even if she's around, because she was so good to us kids; we could stay at the library as long as we wanted and read whatever we wanted.

My desk faces the sea and the islands. I have a good view, despite being in the basement, and it's a nice feeling. I remember the words of the star-master, who said that my work energy was best harnessed in dungeons or secret underground bunkers. And I actually feel good writing here; looking out at the islands eases my mind.

According to the *Saga of Gísli Súrsson*, Ingjaldur's idiot son lived in a turf hut on Hergilsey Island, and Gísli hid there and pretended to be the idiot. I actually dreamed of Auður, Gísli's wife, last night, but I don't remember how she looked; I couldn't

27

see her face, but she handed me a diamond-shaped silver brooch and asked me to keep it safe. According to folklore, dreaming of silver means snow and sorrow, but I had the feeling that my dream meant something else. I called my dear brother, Owlie, and asked him to tell me about Auður; I'd forgotten what happened to her. He said that she'd been a good woman, a good companion of Gísli and faithful to him and that after his death, she'd left the country, gone on a pilgrimage to southern lands.

My dear ornithologist, Birdy, has gone to meet his destiny, living in a cave in the south of Iceland in an attempt to recover his flight feathers. He didn't take his cell phone with him, and it's too far for walkie-talkies. It's probably best to sever all ties in order to reach one's inner divinity, if there is such a thing.

I invited him to come here with me, but he said he preferred not to. He was afraid of digging himself inadvertently into my life or my uterus, saying that he'd felt the desire and thus decided to dig himself into mother earth instead, and then meet me as a new man.

I dreamed of him at dawn; we were in the cave, so deep inside that it was pitch-black and we kissed each other's eyelids and sniffed each other's ears, and then he stroked my hair and slipped into me, which was utterly wonderful. I don't know whether the sound of waves lapping was in my dream or from here on the beach. I woke to the summer solstice feeling blissful, ready to achieve great things.

Under columns full of water from melting glaciers, I dream of justice in this country, yes, and in the world.

I really want fresh fish, but don't know where to get it. The woman at the beauty salon advised me to go down to the harbor when the boats come in and ask the fishermen. I tried, hung around down there but couldn't bring myself to ask. All the fish is sent to Reykjavík and returned frozen for the supermarket. I had a hamburger with béarnaise sauce in the little restaurant by the harbor.

Such crises are like any other period of upheaval, when renewal is closer than ever before. I've been reading an old article by Grandpa in which he harps on about how Icelanders should acquaint themselves better with the ecosystems in and around the country, how the fish live and reproduce. So we don't drive any species to extinction. I've often wished that he were alive, but never more than now; I want to ask him so much about the future.

M ost of the migratory birds have arrived. The plovers line up on the hayfields of the hobby farmers and the whimbrel sings Bach's *Preludes*. I've been drawing for the fun of it. Trying to draw a house. Also made an attempt to draw up a social order, an organic connection of independent clusters. I don't know how self-explanatory my diagram is, but it's definitely ambitious. In a crisis such as this, however, the search for a place of my own merges with my search for a new social structure. In both cases, the question is how to live self-sufficiently, while at the same time in meaningful relationships with others.

I recall the time that I spent on Rue de l'Hermitage, when I'd put so much effort into finding a place of quietude, renting an apartment and retrieving the keys from the end of the world, only to come down with mono. I decided to try to make the best of the situation, and focused on answering, once and for all, the question of the best possible mode of living. Let my mind wander and tried to find a plant that would symbolize my home and lifestyle, my emotional life. Felt as if the violet might do the trick. But now I've discovered that violets grow best beneath big trees, in shadow, and in churchyards, so it's best that I find another flower. I also drew geometric forms: lines, triangles, quadrangles, pentangles, hexagons, heptagons, octagons, but all for nothing; I didn't come to any conclusion. Drew circles with my crappy ballpoint pen.

Then that pictorial teddy bear, Rupert, called and said that he'd come from Amsterdam to Paris and had some drawings that he wanted to show me. He came over, wearing a yellow scarf. He laid a huge white sheet of paper on the table in the kitchen at L'Hermitage, described to me the golden angle and explained with hand gestures how three-dimensionality is created. Is it possible to move into that endlessness? I asked, and he nodded, shook his berry box and said yes, it's entirely possible; it's where I live. I wanted to move in with him. Maybe I was a bit dumbfounded by how attractive a teddy bear he was, and he offered me blueberries, but said he didn't know the address, and had to rush off, besides; he had a meeting with a professional in the creation of forms.

He forgot his scarf. It had a sweet seaweed smell, so I tied it around my drawings, which were rolled up like bark from the sea.

I recall that after he left, I prepared for an oral exam. The other day I had a look back at the textbook, and was rather shocked to see how emphatically I'd underlined the following sentence, in pencil: *Language is the house of Being.*

I'm sure I've been damaged by philosophy. But this just won't do any longer; I simply must take up the ax and plow or whatever it is you take up if you want to protect yourself! A hammer and sickle? A cross and crowbar? Blade and point? At least it's good to remember to try to save yourself while you're saving the country. Isn't it a kind of extravagance to try to save the country before you have solid ground beneath your feet? I remember Mom talking sometimes about extravagance; I didn't quite know what it was, but I had the feeling that it was fairly ambiguous.

W hat's up with that man of yours? Is he ever going to crawl out of that cave, stand up straight?

The archaeologist arrived yesterday morning, warlike in a new leather coat, waxed and winged. He came with outstretched hands, holding a bag of warm croissants.

I was sleepy and hardly in a joking mood, felt the need to defend my man in his cave from this crowing. Not everyone has the courage to give themselves to solitude and look themselves in the eye, as he is doing. I know that he'll be reborn; I trust him completely. Oh, do you really? he asked, before launching into the story of the seven men who secluded themselves in a cave in Ephesus in the Byzantine Empire and slept there for two hundred years until some young girls discovered them and enticed them out. I really must learn their trick. But I wonder what the men dreamed that whole time? You really must find out before taking the next step, he said with a grin, so ironic that it made me think of Skarphéðinn as I brewed us coffee and warmed some milk. Shouldn't you tie your shoe? I asked, making us even.

We sat on the lawn and drank coffee. He invited me to come with him to Hergilsey, where our man Gísli Súrsson hid back in the day; he and some other archaeologists are going to do research on some sites there. He also wants to introduce me to his new girlfriend, who'll be heading out to the island tonight.

We sailed out there, reminiscing on our fondness for Gísli and Auður, how we used to pretend to be them; he was him and I her. Mom sewed tunics for us, and Dad made us swords and shields, so we could defend ourselves in our exile.

Here we are, each in our own tent. It's impossible to go outside, wind and rain; seems like the tents can barely withstand the strain. He said he was going to gather some rocks to shore up the tentpoles. He's restless; doesn't know whether the others can make it out here, which would also mean that we're stuck. He's worried about his girlfriend. I'm also a bit anxious, because I have to send some messages. Thought that my 3G dongle would work.

Hergill Button-butt lived here. His son Ingjaldur kept his own son, called "Ingjaldur's idiot," in an enclosed area called Fíflsgerði (Idiot's Hedge) or Ingjaldsbyrgi (Ingjaldur's Enclosure). In those days, the inhabitants of the island fished and processed the bounty of the sea, engaged in agriculture and grew vegetables. The land there might not have been the best for farming, but the island offered many other benefits.

The remains of five excellent vegetable plots have already been recorded, along with irrigation trenches. It's known that on Oddbjarnarskeri Reef, which I can see in the fog, there were numerous fishing huts. Presumably, the place was quite lively in the spring and fall.

M y brother came to my tent with smoky whiskey in a silver container; oh, apparently it's called a hip flask. He managed to reach the others by telephone and warned them about the weather. They were going to spend the night in Stykkishólmur. We both regretted coming here ahead of them, feeling we'd jumped the gun; otherwise we could have put them up at my place.

We talked a bit about breathing room. I tried to encourage him not to rush too quickly into cohabiting again, and he said that he actually wanted to spend some time by himself, in a vacuum or blank space. Still, he suspected that he would move in with someone sooner rather than later. He would need to transport the blank space piece by piece into the shared space. I told him that I'd given up on it, after all those amazing times that I lived with someone ended in ruins. I'd always felt suffocated.

Next I want to try living apart together, live in the same country, the same city, even the same building as whomever I'm in a relationship with, yet in a different apartment than him. Then it would be possible to pay him visits and still invite good friends over to my place. Do you think you have what it takes to maintain such a French arrangement? he asked. Well, no, probably not . . . but then again . . . ? Maybe it would be better in the long run to stay in a more lasting relationship and not need to move so often.

Don't you want to have a child or children? he then asked. Sure, I replied. You should maybe look into it. For many years, he's advised me not to put it off too long, because it's the most remarkable thing you can do in this life. Yes, yes, I really hope I have the good fortune.

But where's the cradle supposed to be in this LAT relationship, in your apartment or your lover's? Who's going to watch over the child? Sometimes it can keep you awake all night. Won't one of the apartments simply turn into a kind of penalty box before long? he asked. Penalty box? I didn't understand the question. Yes, where one of the lovers hangs out if an argument comes up.

I felt the LAT idea dwindle in my mind. Or did I? Can't a couple take turns watching over the baby? Does everyone always need to be on duty at the same time? No, maybe not. It's hard to say, he said. It's good to divide up and take turns, but you've also always got to be there for your partner. It's so complicated. How the blazes can you have your own space or privacy in such a situation? Unfortunately, I think it's impossible, he said melancholically, taking a big drink.

Were people hospitable out here in the islands? I was excited to hear all about this life, but his description was so melodic that I dozed off, as I did when Dad read *Njál's Saga* to us. In a drowsy haze I envisioned life on the islands, caught snatches of words: bothy, summer byre, grave mounds, wells, and mills. Spindle whorls?

Spindle whorls were found? But brooches? Celtic brooches? And have you ever found a silver brooch? What was the name again of the woman who rowed her own boat between her island and Stykkishólmur for many years?? She was a heroine, wasn't she? Or really intrepid, anyway. You mean Guðrún of Galtarey?

I was in such a cozy, rockabye state, and he went on with his story despite my dozing off because I begged him; please, tell me more, and forgive me for being such a bad listener. What a luxury, to drink of knowledge as if from a baby's bottle.

Yes yes, and Tove Jansson lived out on Klovharu Island off the coast of Finland, and spent all her summers writing there. With her partner, another female artist. Yes, lovers, islands, and ink. Not to forget the printing press on Hrappsey, which posed a challenge to the see of Hólar's monopoly on printed works . . .

I caught the boat back to Stykkishólmur this morning, desperate for an Internet connection. The others remained out on the island to investigate the housing arrangements of the past.

If I could live on an island with chickens and a printing press and sail ashore with manuscripts and eggs, I'd most likely be happy. Or would drown, like Eggert.

My thoughts go round and round. In a grilled green mosquito coil in turquoise and orange Ephesus, where temples, churches, and mosques stand side by side.

And there he is, Beberuhi, that oddball, prankster, and dwarf, cripple and kiss thief. Hi, ho, will you teach me to play chess? I hardly know how the pieces move, am so lame-legged, and it took me so long to learn to swim. A grizzled horse thief calls it quits. Calls on his shadow-puppet friend, who lives in light and shadow. But he's hounded by himself in the twilight and immediately barks back, brusquely: Nor do I know how the pieces move, and my name isn't Beberuhi, you've got it all mixed up. That was that. My new friend, that rookish life and soul of the party, is so arrogant. Or is just a hunchback leper, a foster child of the moor, a suppressed jack-in-the-magma who runs for shelter inside the city because a train crashed near the outdoor chessboard next to the bathhouse, just as the cockaloric, swaggering archcleric lit himself on fire and an earthquake shook the mosaic-adorned buildings, causing the Carnival to come crashing down like shattered glass.

I've gathered so much knowledge just tonight that I feel wobbly, which may be partly due to my residual seasickness. But now I know everything about the neo-colonialists who plan to conquer the world without anyone noticing.

I sit beneath the Water Museum and send messages into the world in defense of water. Against the pollution of greed.

According to the archaeological index, there are eight wells on the island. Who owns those wells? Who owns the water that flows from them, wishing to run into thirsty mouths?

My dear Eyowl winged her way to me yesterday in the dim obscurity of my thoughts, completely perking me up. We sat in the kitchen and chatted into the evening. Then we took the boat out fishing and caught a few cod. I told her about my grandpa's opinions on overfishing and cottage industries, which were entirely in tune with her main concerns and ours. It's a bit extraordinary to engage in such a dialogue after being alone; I could see how our ideas developed, first one circle, one line, and then somewhat more complex forms, as if they'd always existed but were simply waiting for someone to evoke them. And now they're shimmering in the air and I don't quite know what to do about it. We cleaned our catch, and as it marinated we played four-handed on the little brown harpsichord that's here in the annex. We played *Suite for Two Pianos, Allegro diabolico* by Béla Bartók, who says in his autobiography that his compositions were meant to upend the musical tradition by combining forgotten elements from old peasant culture with his own most personal and innovative sounds.

Strange how quickly everything happened after she came. And even more so after she left. She asked me to join her, and now I've flown over to the mainland.

I'm sitting here at the old mosaic brasserie La Strasbourgeoise, looking at the goddess of justice, who's straddling the top of the train station with her eyes blindfolded and holding a broken lightning bolt in one hand, scales in the other. I bought a *demi* and a copy of *Le Monde* and am waiting for the train to Strasbourg, where I'm going to meet with my sisters-in-arms, and I have the feeling that our meeting will open my eyes to a key issue, that the blindfold covering them will be cut. I always dream of it: that something will open my eyes, and open everything inside me as well.

We held our own parliament of owls, like a conspiracy of ravens: one a mainland or long-eared owl with glasses on her nose and polished nails, another a snowy, island owl wearing a bow tie and a key on a necklace, and the third likely a short-eared or little owl, wearing a hat. Clear is the foreign owl-eye in the gloom of the economic collapse; glistening is the eye of the guest. Can you counter high treason, owl?

We met in a little boat and sailed down one of Strasbourg's canals. The magisterial long-eared owl took the oars and told us first about the struggle for the rights of the landless gypsies. Fixed homes have never been a hallmark of theirs. And the same might be said of the world's businessmen, who, as such, have no fixed residences, are entirely unaccountable to their homelands, live in tax havens and tax-free clouds. As garbage and pollution rain over the rest of us . . .

She pulled so strongly on the oars that we shot through the water, dashing past much larger boats. But where have you come from? And what's on your minds? she asked, laying the oars in the boat for the moment.

We adjusted our hats and collars and carefully explained our mission. The sun shone down strongly on the boat and the water sparkled blindingly. We tried to describe to her how energy was still oozing from Iceland's wounds. We told her our ideas for a new way of harnessing the island's energy, channeling it into its own ecosystem and economy, respecting the cycles of nature and supporting the cause of jústice. The owl had begun rowing again and we made one complete circuit of the city. We returned the boat and wandered into a little café by a bridge.

Let me have a look at your files, she said, adjusting her glasses on her sharp nose. She ran her darting eyes over the numbers and names and said that the case was clearly dripping with corruption. She drew up a diagram for us and I felt as if I gained instant insight into how rotten my country's infrastructure was. And how great a responsibility those bear who refuse to admit it. But we can't mention any names at this stage; the history of this corruption needs to be probed to its core.

Finally, we asked her advice on a referendum and discussed a new democratic structure for the national economy. When we said goodbye, she suggested that we ask the sharp-eyed Hawk for help; he was a former architect and the current mastermind behind the new scheme.

We stood there, tired and thirsty, on the station platform, not knowing which trains to take. Are you heading east? You west? Over the sea again? No, we decided to rest up a bit, prepare ourselves for our migration, get our bearings on the front of the V.

We went to the station restrooms to change clothes. Emerged as lounge lizards, she in a copper-colored dress, I in a red-checkered one, and we dashed to Basel on the evening train, because we knew that there were other lizards here, and not in our way, but in a big room decorated with pencil drawings.

It's good to meet artists when you've read a bit too much about law and economics. Refresh your imagination.

Everyone's worried about the old country. The discussion about Iceland continued into the night. Imagine if our children and grandchildren needed to buy water at a high price from those who took control of the water supply. And to slave away on the crofts of foreign magnates. The country is crumbling beneath us; we must fight now to ensure that its future inhabitants can stand on solid ground and hold their heads high. Rather chieftains than slaves, said someone in German, but I didn't really know if that was the right way to put it. What do we call chieftains when there aren't any more slaves? We become those chieftains. Equals. Here's to that!

We played the fantasy for four hands, which turned into eight and sixteen, and sang *I spotted a curlew down at the bay* as a round and said that we hoped the song would continue, that there would always be someone singing *peep peep peep . . . peep peep, off to sleep . . . doze soft and deep, while watch I keep . . .*

When I woke this morning, I felt like a hooded seal—but with my balloon burst. My ideals lay in tatters on the pillow. I thought about Nietzsche, who was a professor here in Basel and tried to burst through stifling structures but accidentally burst his own mind at the same time, and near the end held imaginary conversations with animals. He'd already renounced his Prussian citizenship, and died a stateless man.

I crawled out to the kitchen in the artists' residence, where my dear Seala is staying for a while, though she says she misses the tides and the saltiness of the sea. She serves her guests the finest rutabaga salad and coffee with milk, more and more of whom crawl out of their dark corners; she puts up as many as she can at such festive times. We sat there until noon talking about space and houses. I said that I thought I'd like to have one house by the sea and another inland. Eyowl then told us about Anaïs Nin's house in California, which is Japanese in style, with a huge studio where she had complete privacy to write. She went there regularly during her years in America, was married to two men and split her time between them, lived in two very different houses. Well now, this certainly surprised me. That she'd lived such a perfectly double life.

Strindberg's little hut is on an island, in a forest, and his desk is still in it, all by itself, said a certain Doggy, making a strong entry into the conversation. Somehow I feel as though the privacy that Strindberg had sought was empty or negative, privacy in a kind of nowhere, because he derived his creative power from solitude and self-pity. On the other hand, I think that Nin sought privacy that was loaded with life and memories, because she seems to have derived her strength from inter-action with others, said Doggy. I don't know if this analysis is correct, but I probably need both: complete solitude and loving interaction. But hopefully my creativity only needs one husband! He's got to be my equal. A man I'm not dependent on and who isn't dependent on me, but who chooses willingly and gladly to be only with me. And of course I would want only to be with him, even if I were to pop over to California sometimes.

I'm on the night train, headed for Gare du Nord.

I arrived in Paris very early in the morning. Had a proper cup of coffee and gut-defying bread with delicious honey at Café Time. Studied the Metro map and planned things out. I had to run to catch my plane home, but did loads of errands beforehand. Retrieved my books from storage (compare: *Manuscripts home! Bones home!*), found a specialty perfumery that sold scent of ivy, and met my dear friend and fellow scholar Moose, who told me the latest from the research community. Together we ate imitation monkey brains and beef tongue braised in red wine.

I had a long phone conversation with Owlie tonight. He told me the surprising news that he'd had such a craving for beef tongue yesterday that he drove a long way to find one, and then cooked it and ate it with mashed potatoes. This telepathy—tonguepathy—left us dumbstruck. And anyway, it's pathetic to crave this sensitive body part of an animal while wanting to protect animals from violence.

Today I walked up Helgafell without looking back, and made a wish as I did so. Looked over the grave of Guðrún Ósvífursdóttir, there where she'd sought quietude at the end of her life. I didn't completely remember how many wishes I was allowed to make, according to tradition, but I decided

47

to make three: one for nature, the second for justice, and the third for love.

I think of the ornithologist. How does he feel in his cave? Is he receiving my telepathic messages? I went for a walk tonight in Stykkishólmur, making my usual circuit. Greeted the cormorants, which sit so sagely on the basalt beach. And I'm not afraid at all of the fulmars anymore; apparently they don't spray stomach oil on you unless you threaten them. They're just old and curious, have seen so much in their long lives that they long to see something new, or at least that's what Birdy said, and I believe everything he says.

I called Hawk and we talked for a long time about the possibility of a referendum on the groundbreaking decisions concerning the future of Iceland's national resources. We're all going to meet here tomorrow.

Now the sun is up again, having dipped into the sea for a second and risen anew, livelier than ever. Elliðaey Island is radiant. I'm going to allow myself to stay up all night and then have dandelion leaves for breakfast, maybe some canned sardines. And read. I'm finishing a book by Leonora Carrington, about an old surrealist woman with a hearing trumpet who lives in a retirement home shaped like a wedding cake; I had it sent express over the sea.

And I've invented a new game: time how long a top can spin at one toss. My record is one minute, twelve seconds. Then it spins in the other direction.

I t's Midsummer Day. I went out into the storm to pick little
flowers to put under my pillow in the hope that I'll dream
of a man in a cave who opens up from the soil like a succulent
flower. According to the almanac, there's also an Eldríður
Day, which seems to be a reference to Æthelthryth, a seventh-
century nun who founded an abbey in Ely in England, and
which was destroyed by Vikings in 870. But who was it that
put this almanac together? I recall mornings in the countryside
with Grandma, when, after serving the tourists breakfast, we'd
sit quietly at the kitchen table, sipping coffee, and one of us
would notice that yesterday's page hadn't been torn from the
calendar. It was such fun to tear off the pages and reveal the
next day's name. The Icelandic almanac appears to be tied to
sheep farming, in part, despite it never mentioning the rutting
or lambing seasons. It also has a few Catholic and Christian feast
days and maybe a pagan festival or two that have come along
for the ride. There must be scholarly articles on the origins of
all the world's feast days. And I should put together my own
almanac, and consult it, of course. My first kiss, first broken
heart, first pang of conscience, first declaration of independence, first complete thought. How does one go about creating
such a calendar?

It's cozy being indoors in the rain. It's the time for meetings, according to the almanac. Today we held our bird meeting, talked things over and rubbed our beaks together. We aren't imps, but birds flying in a beautiful V-formation. Made a plan to encourage the nation to let its voice be heard.

Now I'm chatting with myself in solitude, calming myself down after the hullabaloo; we discussed so much, with such passion, and drew up countless possible paths to take, apart from the ones now being taken without consent from the nation. It can be so exhausting, trying to come up with ideas on what would be best for the nation. I wonder how it feels to have to do it as a full-time job? All the idealists—do they die burned out? I stare at the sea and listen to the rain pound the waves, water on water.

When the wet, blood-red sun had disappeared behind the islands, I watched *The Lives of Others* and cried my eyes out. Remembered what my friend had said after the fall of the Iron Curtain, that she'd stopped trusting her friends. Friendships in ruins. In the system of universal trust and unispatial closeness.

What did he call himself again, the Hungarian professor? A dog? Said that he'd invented animal names for everyone he knew during the totalitarian period, when everything was under surveillance. I waited excitedly for him to say my name—and finally it was my turn to be called into the animal kingdom: *Greetings and may good fortune ever come your way, Teddy Bear*. Later, I received a long, poetic letter that began with the salutation, *Good day to you, Teddy Bear Queen*.

I can't sleep. Hear the hoofbeats of an old satyr. It dashes in from the horizon and leans on me, panting.

Are you surprised you're all alone, crazy old Teddy Bear? Remember when you were going to blow up your unhappiness, and accidentally blew up everything instead? Time bombs are always wrongly timed. And lying pollutes your inner lakes; the clouds turn gray from anxiety.

It was a holiday and I'd prepared everything so well, wanted to be impeccably hospitable, but because I'd heard someone say something untrue earlier in the evening and didn't want to start the new year with things left unreckoned from the old one, so much tension was generated that it was as if lightning blasted me in the head. I blew up just before the fireworks were set off. The truth or life.

A black, scorched ring formed around me, and no one dared enter it. Except for my brother. He's an expert on ruins, stepped in over the line, put his arms around me and said he understood me.

I've been thinking about this step. How big it is. When someone comes and lays a conciliatory hand on a wound.

Mom came to me whenever I felt bad, and I remember when I realized that I could do the same, go to her. She lay on the couch, tired after her attempt to lighten the mood in the house. I didn't know whether she wanted to be alone, and felt as if there were a blue veil enveloping her. I was afraid of this veil. I thought I would never get through it, and even if I did, then what? But I decided to slip through the invisible membrane and she was happy to have me close. We went out into the yard together and decided on a place to put a little shed.

I think that in the housing of the future, there needs to be a little healing nook where you can lie down as if under the grass or down in the ground and let the earth restore you. Then rise up. Christianity is perhaps first and foremost an admonition to ground yourself so well that the light can play around you without burning you up, an admonition to connect with nature, turn to dust each day and rise up from the dust, transcend the laws of nature with help from the laws of nature. You mustn't bury yourself alive, forget to rise up, or bind yourself to the dust in melancholy surrender.

I was starting to grow antsy. There'd been no news from the cave for a very long time. I looked in the mailbox five times a day, couldn't help it. Then this morning the mail carrier came strolling up the dandelion slope, with a sarcastic look on her face, which made me think she might have something for me, and sure enough, she handed me a postcard, perhaps having read it already, which is fine; postcards are public by nature. No one's so poor that he can't get himself an envelope. Written on the card was the message: *I'm on my way to you, will you come meet me?*

At first I acted as if nothing were out of the ordinary; I just roasted some eggplant and perused a book, but then threw some stuff into a suitcase and ran like fire to catch the bus, sat down panting at the very back. Now there's a short stop at Vegamót, and I've bought myself some licorice and soda water.

Thankfully, the driver is old-fashioned and has the radio tuned to Channel 1, and no one's talking on their cell phones. I'm sitting next to a man who has told me all about the brewery where he works, brewing organic beer from Icelandic barley, though it's on the verge of bankruptcy. Previously, he was a nursery grower but it was difficult to make ends meet; electricity is cheaper for big industry than for greenhouses, and the distribution system is so screwed up that a huge amount of vegetables and fruit have to be thrown out to keep the market price high. I just don't get it. When is economics going to renew itself and come up with new theories? Wasn't there a turning point? Wasn't everything supposed to change? I'm so impatient, and the glacier is melting fast. Those wretched district-council members who thought they were making a great deal when they sold the tycoon access to the water from the glacier for a hundred years, believing all his promises about development in the district, only to see him sitting in jail for tax evasion and forgery. Rather hard, if the land has to be sold off in pieces and the water supply polluted before the scoundrels are put behind bars. They're still on the loose, with their long bankruptcy- and swindle-tails. On the other hand, you've got to have a clean criminal record to get a license to drive a moped. But anyway, the bus has just jerked into motion. I say farewell to the glacier, regretfully, but not sadly.

I borrowed the car from Pa and Ma and went to meet him,
since he'd decided to leave his cave. I met him in Hveragerði,
and his feet were in bad shape. But he was in a joyous mood, had
met a lot of birds along the way, hiked over marshlands when
the sands ended. St. Christopher ferried him over the rivers.
I was so happy to see him that I acted shy and impersonal. I
asked him professionally and thoroughly about his hike, as if
I were interviewing him on the radio, and only then did we
hug each other.

Went to a pharmacy to buy bandages and antiseptic. Sat
down by a bubbling hot spring and he let me treat his wounds,
hesitantly at first, but then he relaxed and leaned back. I'm so
happy to sense how well grounded he is. Like a new man. And
he said, like Jóhann Sigurjónsson wrote in a verse in response
to hardship: *I'm wearing new socks and I'm wearing new shoes. In
all the world there's no one I fear.*

We let poetry decide, went to the nearest store and he
bought himself shoes—black moccasins. I found it a very odd
choice; he probably won't get used to such shoes. I felt unusually
skeptical about them but pulled myself together, let go of my
fear. Are these the shoes of tyrants? The shoes of Freemasons?
I stepped aside and called Grandma, asked her what kind of

shoes Grandpa wore and she said that he'd always worn shoes with laces and that he hadn't been a Freemason.

Subsequently, we made an even more momentous decision than we could have anticipated: to get ice cream—dipped cones, no less.

The woman who served us was in her forties and tattooed, cool patterns behind her ear and on her shoulder, and she had eyes like a seal's. She never takes time off, she told us, and the shop was full of children that she chatted to as if they were adults.

As we licked our ice-cream cones, we walked across the parking lot and noticed that the upper floor of the building that was once the town's health clinic was for rent. We looked in through the window and saw an empty green space with a beautiful spiral staircase with a wooden handrail. On the spot, we decided to move there together, without having a good look at the place or asking about terms.

Our decisions are peculiar: I found it difficult to decide whether I wanted a dipped cone or a regular one, but had no trouble at all deciding to move house over the heath.

I called the woman who owned the house and she told me it would be free in January, and we could move in then if we liked.

After the call, I had second thoughts—what if I got pregnant and had an insatiable craving for ice cream, like so many women? It would be so easy to fill—I would just hang around at the shop getting fatter and fatter, and he would cross the heath to Reykjavík and not come back, and I would be alone with a small child who would be raised partly down at the shop.

You scaredy-cat, you nervous Nelly, as if you wouldn't just get a cool tattoo and be a studly single mother, licking her ice cream.

We can't move into the apartment across the heath until the New Year. We didn't think we'd be able to find another place in the meantime, but my brother and I were offered the opportunity to rent an apartment together for several months, and we took it. It's a good interim measure. My nephews stay with us from time to time.

Mom's birthday was yesterday and we held a waffle party out in the yard; the weather was good and the wasps were lively. Grandma came too, and was so funny that I thought Mom and I would pee our pants. Birdy encouraged me to play a tune on the organ and said nice things about it, even though I didn't have my glasses and messed up every other note. I miss having a piano in the kitchen. He said he hoped we'd have room for instruments in our future home. We've decided to live together someday. But until then, we're going to try living apart together. We take out the walkie-talkies. He's still living in the same place, along with a few silverfish, which he's befriended, saying that they're prehistoric and quite beautiful under certain lighting conditions.

Owlie and I invited everyone over to have a look at our new home, which is still in boxes, and it was fun seeing them inspect the place. Grandma asked about the water, whether the cold water was cold and the hot water hot, while Mom contemplated the arrangement of space and sniffed around, giving the bathroom a suspicious glance. Dad knocked on the wall and wondered how soundproof it was, whether we could play music without disturbing the neighbors.

They brought a housewarming gift: a new, beautifully bound edition of the Icelandic sagas. To read aloud to my little nephews, raise the next generation. They said they were glad to know that my brother and I were sharing the place; we'd always been good to each other and now it was important to stand together and make a nice home for the boys after the divorce.

They're coming tomorrow and will stay a few days. They'll be in the bedroom. My brother is staying in the living room, and I in a corner room with boxes of books and clothing on the floor; I've got to get myself a cabinet or trunk. Need a reading lamp, too.

The dear brothers come now and then to my room, to have a look at my things and chat. Just now, they asked me why couples divorce. They said they didn't understand it. I had to admit that I didn't understand it either, but tried to explain things to those sweet pups. They lap up every word, so I have to be careful what I say.

After this, they asked about violence. They're worried about the way teenagers are violent to each other and are already nervous about becoming teenagers themselves. I wanted to tell it like it is, that they were right: it's nerve-wracking being a teenager. But instead, I explained to them the importance of being a trusted friend, and that friendship made the teenage years fun, when true camaraderie grew and developed.

Having trusted friends isn't actually a given. Friendship has to be watered, like a delicate plant; that's what your dad always said. They were worried about their parents' friends; what would happen to them after the divorce. We'll see, I said. They were very wise and told me stories from school, about friends who'd stopped being friends, about others who were inseparable, always together, and about some who seemed not to want any friends. I said I doubted that there were people who didn't want friends. If there were, it was probably just a defense mechanism—they were likely afraid of not being good friends themselves, or afraid that no one wanted to be their friend.

They said that their dad was a good friend; they could tell him everything. I agreed; he truly is a good friend. Then they went to bed, and I read one chapter of an Icelandic saga to them. They know *Njál's Saga* by heart, having listened to it so often in the car. They call dibs on being Kári or Gunnar. Ask me who my favorite is. I haven't decided.

The apartment's only openable window is in my room, and I let my little brother, the honorable father of two, come in sometimes to smoke at it. He came earlier, after the boys were asleep. Sat down here on the bed and we had a little chat about things.

He asked about my LAT partner, was excited to hear more about him. Said that he felt like he was also in love with him, in sympathy with me, sympathetic joy. Maybe you two ought to get together, instead, I said, feeling as if sharing him might be a good solution. Are you sure you couldn't love a man? I asked. He laughed and reminded me that I'd already asked him that several times, and added that I wasn't the only one who'd done so.

He said that so far, he'd only loved women sexually, but had, on the other hand, loved some men very deeply, but in a different way. He told me, for example, that for several years he'd had a feeling about this particular fellow of mine; thought he seemed nice, sympathetic. And he, like I do, thinks we're a good match. Maybe we feel that way because he resembles you a bit, I said. No, he didn't agree. But then maybe he's too similar to me? I asked.

Couldn't it be difficult living with another writer? Doesn't he write just in his spare time? he asked. Yes, that's what he does now, but he's planning to turn to writing full time. So he'd be competing with you, then, as a writer; in which case, it might be best for you to make a run for it, he said sagely.

We agree that competition in love and friendship is a very bad thing. He's trying hard to instill in his sons something other than a competitive spirit, but to no avail: they're always competing with each other. Why are we so opposed to competition? I asked him. Then the phone rang, his new woman was on the line, and he went to the living room.

I've always respected how he's never acted jealous, even when I was getting far more attention for a time, as the big sister. He just showed solidarity, saying that it wasn't always easy being a clown, as I'd ended up.

I remember a movie I saw about a little clan in Mongolia, in which women live with their brothers in peace and harmony. The fathers of their children and their lovers come visit them, bringing their children coats, for example, and walking them to school. I don't remember quite what was so good about this arrangement, except, yes, that it seems to have been free from violence. The men who were brothers were awesome and helped as much as they could with the householding, while the men who were fathers were pretty much losers. Their wives didn't expect much from them.

I've never been afraid of being too close to my brother. Admittedly, as a teenager I was worried that it was unnatural to miss him so much and to fear constantly that something might happen to him. And he said that he once felt a bit odd, wanting to be so close to his friends and family. Why do we want that? he asked me. Probably because we were raised to be close, I said. Isn't it a bit greedy to always want that? he asked. Yes, of course, I replied, and we decided to be careful.

In any case, I need to be careful not to use our closeness as a weapon against anyone I'm in a relationship with. As if the intimacy that developed could never measure up to the unconditional love between me and my brother. I don't recall ever having done it deliberately, although I might have taken shelter under the wing of brotherly love when I feared betrayal and loneliness. Yes, probably. Shame on me.

The other day it dawned on me that all the men I lived with became a bit jealous of my relationship with my brother. And maybe the women in his life were to some extent uncomfortable, too, I don't know.

Of course, you've got to be cautious not to let an unconditional love swamp your intimacy with others, especially if they're sensitive or insecure. But I find it strange that pure love can be a destructive force. I guess it is, though, sometimes. Maybe I'm making a grave mistake by living with my brother. Typical when you think you're doing the right thing, that you're above reproach! *The road to hell is paved with good intentions*, said the medieval monk, before gulping down an entire cask of red wine.

He said he'd noticed, to his great sorrow, that his sons' laughter wasn't as uninhibited as before; now they tried to act manly, and smirked. Maybe they listen too much to *Njál's Saga*; and was it stupid of me to say that my favorite character is Skarphéðinn? he asked, sunk in thought. I then remembered when my brother himself stopped laughing his joyful, curly laughter that flowed in light waves, and I'm pretty sure that *Njál's Saga* wasn't to blame.

Then a long-forgotten memory took him completely by surprise. It was his first year in school in Reykjavík and he'd sensed that his exuberance wasn't appreciated; then some girls made faces when he laughed and burst into laughter themselves, nastily, and tried to mimic him. He decided, at that instant, to stop laughing like an idiot. He was seven years old.

I also remembered one recess at the start of the school year, when he stood by himself against the gray concrete wall in a blue down coat, turned his face to the wall and spoke not a word. I went and said something to him but he gave me a sign with one foot that he didn't want to talk. I felt a piercing pain in my heart and watched him from a distance. And saw, when he turned around, that his defenses were up.

I don't remember ever being bullied at school. I always got to take part in the games even though I wore thick glasses and had freckles, since my teacher, Sveinbjörn, was so good and paid close attention to all the pupils and took immediate action at the slightest instance of bullying, and discussed it with us. However, I also remember not understanding the rules of the games and not wanting to take part, finding them boring and pointless. Sometimes my brother and I left the schoolyard to chat and see if there was anything interesting in the garbage lying around.

Maybe we just didn't understand how competitive it was. Because in rural schools, there weren't enough pupils to divide into teams. None of the pupils were the same age; we were all grouped together into one class and the teachers urged us not to worry about the others, but to set our own goals and try to achieve based on our own abilities. That was Fjöll Municipality Elementary School, when both it and that municipality still existed. Dad and Mom taught us everything except music; for that, we went over to Grandma's, who played the organ, and learned from her the most popular folk songs and hymns. Then we would go with Grandpa to the sheep sheds, where he taught us how to conduct ourselves around sheep without spooking them.

Then came the student teacher, who had obviously checked off the box about teaching in the smallest school in Iceland. He introduced us to the latest theories in psychology and talked about the bullying cycle, which is harmful to everyone, both the perpetrators and victims. Dad and Mom put a lot of emphasis on finding ways to break the cycle of violence. Or perhaps not to break anything, but rather, just to step out of the ring.

As soon as we arrived in town, we were subject to a pretty violent beating. It was outside the City Library and the boys were wearing cleats, and they shoved me and Owlie down into the snow and kicked us in the stomach. Did we have some sort of thin countryside aura around us—no hardened city countenance? Do those who come from the countryside always have the shit beaten out of them? Dad never told us, until in passing the other day, that when he finally started attending public school, he got in a lot of fights. Until then, his education had come from itinerant teachers.

My brother and I were invited to take judo lessons, to learn how to use our enemies' strength to our advantage. It was really fun to learn something physical, and I always pictured an *ippon* whenever I thought some savage teenagers were approaching. But the competitive aspect sucked, and we decided to quit because of it. It wasn't enough to learn the moves; you had to take part in tournaments. But we didn't want to compete—just to play. The teacher was sorry about it, said that was how the system worked, unfortunately. So we quit; stepped out of the ring that was supposed to help us step out of the ring.

My shepherd and friend of birds turned up unexpectedly last night, knocked on our door and was given a warm welcome. We kissed our guest, and the man of the house opened a first-rate bottle of whiskey and poured glasses for us. We'd been discussing our elementary-school years and asked him about his experience, whether he'd ever been beaten in Breiðholt. He declared that in his memory elementary school was hell. In his school, a few boys controlled everything and everyone according to some incomprehensible rules. On his first day, he was beaten up; same for his second day, and his third day too. I asked if he'd grown accustomed to it, if perhaps he'd even wanted to be beaten—otherwise why was it still happening? The other day someone attacked him at random on the street. Of course, my questions were imprudent and inappropriate. But he didn't seem to mind.

He's staying here tonight. He's sleeping beneath the lamp, but I'm going to write a bit longer, sitting at my desk, listening to his breathing.

He undresses so professionally, and I asked him about his skull-shaped belt buckle. It's a rare bird of prey, he explained.

Owlie and Birdy both have such belts, and the little boys want exactly the same sort, with the same sort of buckle. With a picture of a wolf's head or a sneaky, poisonous snake. These are the shields of sweet darlings, protectors of little birds and tittering waders.

M om and I went for a long drive and discussed things. Had a look at houses along the way. I asked her whether it had been tough to build our house—which seemed to be forever under construction. Sure, for a time it was hard, but it's so much fun to nurture a house that's living, constantly changing. Houses, like bodies, always require maintenance. You're never completely finished creating a home. It's best to see it as an eternal project. I found it strange and comforting to witness this serene dauntlessness of hers. I recall having thought, since it took my parents so endlessly long to finish their house, that it would be so difficult to build my own that I would never attempt it. But it's probably even harder not having a house.

I told her that I couldn't imagine being a worry-free mother. She said that you gradually learn to let go; incredible but true. Then she asked whether I wanted to create my own home with my boyfriend. She said that it was no use waiting for trust to come to you fully formed, and then go and create a life and home together; you just had to start living with the person you loved best, and trust would build over time.

We went to Grandma's for coffee and asked her to describe the places where she'd lived during her life, the spaces that she'd had to herself. She was game, and delivered her description systematically and enthusiastically, beginning with the old-style living room where she was born and where she lay like a little sailboat, listening to the chickens on the roof. Then she described the attic that was her and her sisters' private domain, where there were windows facing the sea. Then her own bedroom in her parents' house in the north, and the little room she rented with her girlfriend. Then her room at the housewife school and the other rooms in Reykjavík, the little kitchenette and sewing room where she spent a lot of time. And the bird room on the twentieth floor of the copper tower in New York. She said that she'd had a good view everywhere. Like now—apart from her window facing away from Mt. Esja.

It appears that, as an adult, she never had a room of her own until she became a widow. On the other hand, her grandmother, who lived with them in her childhood home, had her own room, whose door she opened at certain times of day. Then everyone would want to come in, look out her window, listen to stories and while away the time.

It was fifty years ago today that I found the spearhead among the ruins at home, said Dad, before adding that an archaeologist from Reykjavík had come and examined it respectfully and said that it was a Viking spear. We were always hoping that it would be put on display in the National Museum, but it's probably still lying in a safe place in storage somewhere. Dad fought all the snowdrifts with ancient-looking sticks. But after he found a real weapon, his interest shifted to the sciences. He remembers how the archaeologist who came north sat sagely on the couch in the evening, reading a book.

I want to get the chance to read Dad's old diaries; they're in the Þingeyjar Co-op box in the basement. He joked that I would be allowed to read his diaries when he was allowed to read mine. But he said that all he'd really written were private observations on the weather, like the old farmhand who would take himself off to his little cubbyhole to write about elves and storms, sitting on his cot with the book on his knees. I'm sure you can get insight into people's emotional struggles from their descriptions of the weather.

I've rarely seen Dad angry, but yesterday I heard him chew out a man who'd advertised his little turf hut as a bungalow for tourists. Dad has insisted that the hut be open to all, and that all who pass by are welcome to use it as needed. But for some unscrupulous salesman to offer it without permission and not even apologize . . . I thought Dad would have a heart attack.

Today is my boyfriend's birthday. I'm going to go downtown and buy him something nice, maybe binoculars and Sveinbjörn Beinteinsson's book on metrics, though I'm afraid he already has it—I think I've seen it on his shelf. He's a clever versifier and I really want to train myself in it; then we could bandy verses someday. I'm also going to give him the old grave index that Grandpa gave me. It's big and black, with blood-red corners, but there's nothing registered in it—just empty spaces for the corpses of the future. It's appropriate for him to have it, since he was born on the Day of the Dead. Owlie and I are going to cook the blood pudding that we made and invite the birthday boy to dinner. Maybe we'll listen to old death-metal cassettes in the basement apartment tonight. And talk about life and the future. My brother and I will lose the apartment soon. Question of whether I take a giant step and buy an apartment. Or a farm. Whether I'll start doing a better job of providing for myself and stop living month-to-month like an old rheumatic line dancer in a circus. We could still rent the apartment in Hveragerði, which might be a good solution for now. And then of course we'll start thinking about flooring and plumbing. And when we do, it's going to be fun.

The last few days I've been up to my ears in matters of societal and national interest, and it's going pretty well. But it takes so much perseverance and precision to pursue issues that are constantly pushed aside in the collective debate. You start feeling like a demon that they've tried to exorcise, but that rears its head again and again, cackling and howling. Some ears are full of corruption and rémoulade. Luckily, there are quite a few demons, taking turns trying to be heard.

O wlie had a job interview this morning and was going directly from his archaeological excavation, all dirty and wearing an old leather coat. I pointed out that it might upset some people to have their floors dirtied in the middle of the day. Envisioned professional behavior analysts putting an X next to "Applicant's style" and writing the following comment: "Dirty, with an earring, necklace, and tattoos." So he put on a nice jacket and a checkered wool tie.

I've often been told that my brother is studly. I used to get defensive on his behalf; didn't understand what people meant. And he wouldn't admit to it himself. What exactly is that? Arrogant? No, not arrogant, more like effortless. What makes a person studly?

I think I find men most studly when they're so confident of their own masculinity that they can allow themselves to be playful with it and develop their feminine sides. But where does that confidence and playfulness come from? From the earth or the sky? From the moon? Could it be that studliness streams down into the heads of those who are open to a bigger context than their own egos, yet who manage to let it flow through them and thus experience themselves as part of a broader context? Maybe men need to be both grounded and ungrounded, with their calves dirty from kicking up the dirt, but their minds wise and humble, in touch with the cycles of nature. This connection is very different from the anchorage found in some men and women, who've tied their tails to the system and revolve on the eternal wheel of power, while considering themselves independent and hip. They smarm their way in and then go around threatening and bribing people. But then their tails suddenly get wet. When the deep opens, the swell is fierce.

I agreed to deliver a lecture on renewal and alchemy for a small group of enthusiastic women in a continuing education course. I was offered a good sum for it and felt I'd really caught a lucky break just before Christmas. I prepared myself well, wanting to bring a new perspective to these energetic women who I'd been told were democracy-loving.

I was to meet them in a mysterious house by the Pond; I found the choice of location unusual but didn't think more about it, was the first one there and suddenly had stage fright, drank coffee, munched down a piece of chocolate cake and went over the main points of my lecture. Then they came in, fashionably dressed, tails cocked, and shook my hand firmly, looked me straight in the eye and asked if I was the one who was going to tell them all about my crazy book writing. Maybe they were joking, but I didn't laugh, and didn't know what to say. I was surprised to see them, too. Because they turned out to be notorious jackals, strategic and shrewd, and had played an active part in sinking the national ship, unashamedly knocking a hole in its hull. Now they pretended to be working for the public interest, which they said they'd always been trying to do, but were simply hampered so much by the global economic crisis.

*

I'm so ticked off at myself for not getting up and walking out. I remember thinking that I couldn't be sure, maybe they were the best people to right the ship, their regret probably so deep that they were open to a complete mental rebirth. So I delivered my lecture, placing great emphasis on participatory democracy and public property, but then one of them said: Sorry, but I've come to the conclusion that people are idiots.

Yes, you might say that. At least I am. To believe that you, you "promising, young" upstarts, could have any sense of shame; that you could, through repentance, approach humility, I thought.

Now, you're a creative person, one of them remarked toward the end. Would you say you use both hemispheres of your brain at once to think? I don't remember my reply; my mind was a black hole. Gave them a courteous goodbye and went out into the sleet.

I don't know whether it's because I'm in my thirties or because of the spirit of the season or the coming holiday, but I find myself thinking about friendship more than usual. I feel as if I'm seeing everything in a new light. The lines become clearer: I have things in common with some people, with others not. I don't think that saying such a thing implies any judgment. More like a kind of realism, or whatever you want to call it. But that doesn't change the fact that your relationships with those who are on the same path need to be reconstructed at every single crossroad.

Tonight, Owlie and I have been tidying and wrapping presents and talking about various things from our teenage years. As it turns out, our relationship hasn't always been so good. For a number of years, maybe ten, we were quite distant. I felt like I needed to let him be. And I think that he'd wanted to be free of my psychological conjectures, when I was seeing a therapist and started analyzing our relationships with our dad and mom and so on. He wasn't ready for it. But then, one day it happened; I remember that we were walking in Brooklyn, and he asked about my psyche.

Talking about this tonight, I recalled my joy at our reunion. As if our souls had met and reconciled. Strange to have forgotten it, almost as if we take our relationship for granted now, when it's so good.

At the same time, I recalled what I thought on the way home from our walk. Thought that I should be careful not to be too pleased by our conversation and to respect the time that had passed, to avoid thinking that we'd gone back in time and that our roles hadn't changed. I don't need to be the worried, bossy sister. I've got to learn to play with him in a new way. I get an excellent chance to practice every time he comes to my room to smoke out the window.

I'd witnessed his night sweats and heard his voice break, when he talked like a goose. I was delighted to see what a fine man he was turning out to be. But I was so disappointed when I saw him light up a filterless Gitanes, or was it a Gauloises, I don't remember the brand precisely; at least he smoked cigarettes that I knew Dad had praised most and said were the very best. When we came home and were alone, I asked him if he couldn't be more original; if he had to follow blindly in Dad's footsteps. He said that it had nothing to do with that.

Are you going to fester in an adolescent body that's already begun to rot prematurely? Don't you want to keep developing?

I remember when he tried yet another time to quit smoking, but I advised him to wait, to avoid making the same mistake as Dad, who decided to quit just before we went on a trip and was in a bad mood the entire time, cursing the idiot tourists. Naturally, it's never good to urge people to try to outdo their fathers; it just raises multiple defenses, first for their fathers, and then for themselves. And finally he got so angry with me that he simply hung up. Called shortly afterward to announce that he'd decided to smoke again, and told me, after pausing to take a drag on his first cigarette, that he found nothing more painful than arguing with me. And I realized that I could say the same thing.

Still, we've attempted to argue when necessary; you've got to be able to let loose and even lose your temper a bit if you're finding it hard to breathe. Closeness has to be like running water; it mustn't stagnate and sour.

I skated numerous rings around the little islet and the big one too, and the kids were with me and we did all sorts of tricks, practiced skating backwards. We had hot chocolate on the bank and rested our ankles, then dashed out to make another ring, and went round and round.

Owlie and Birdy went hunting ptarmigan together. Returned home empty-handed, but happy. They laughed a lot and teased each other—Birdy made fun of Owlie's fear of skuas and Owlie of Birdy's ambivalence toward firearms, asking when he was going to make up his mind about the validity of killing ptarmigan. Then they blamed their glasses; both of them had such old lenses that nothing was in focus, and they'd simply shot one snowdrift after another. Although ptarmigan is the tastiest thing of all, we feel it ought to be declared protected.

They rolled themselves cigarettes and asked whether there was any holiday drink around. I was emptying the picnic bag, and yes indeed, what should I find there but a flask of bitters. Then they noticed our skating outfits and laughed at how we looked. Is that supposed to be a coverall? Did the kids find it fun to be with such a goofball?

We've always been able to laugh about it, me and Owlie, whenever I've dressed myself weirdly. It's something genetic.

He never put his sweater on inside out, whereas I often did. And when I was a teenager and wanted to make a strong impression at a school party, I dug through all my clothes and his and even got to try on all of Mom's clothes, but ended up heading out in one of Dad's outfits, leaving everything at home a complete mess. Owlie wasn't a teenager then, and he got a good laugh out of it. It can be funny to relive the leap that you made from childhood to the adult that you are now. Because when the leap fails, and you have to crawl like a fool out of the ditch, you can often see your adult persona in hindsight, how ridiculous when it takes itself too seriously in its costume, its skirt dripping with mud.

In romantic relationships, there are generally limits to how often you can make a fool of yourself. I probably need to try to be more confident, throw on some leather boots and leap out into the day. Or what? Maybe you've got to have enough leeway in a romantic relationship to be able to leap from childish foolishness to adult seriousness and laugh about it. To be both cool and a lame idiot.

They pulled out packages, one marked "The Knitting Shop," which contained a pair of the finest mittens, from Birdy. The other was marked "Compound Feed Shop" and contained riding breeches, from Owlie. I'd dreamed of having such breeches when I was a teenager, but was sure I wouldn't fit in them—my butt was too big. These have a Ruskin seat and fit me perfectly.

I put on makeup and cooked us a birthday stew. They both said that my breeches looked good on me, which, I must admit, made me very happy. And I found them both very studly in their hunting outfits.

I t's much better to work at home and be able to start writing before you get dressed, before you start discussing things with this person or that. I'm glad to have moved out of Reykjavík, feeling as if we left the stress behind when we moved over the heath. There's more peace and quiet here.

It took quite a long time to move all of our stuff out of storage. I was also teaching and busy with various other things, so I haven't been able to write in my diary since we moved. I also think that people write less in diaries and "dreamaries" when they're in love. But now the good old tranquility of the short, dark winter days has settled into my bones.

I baked for my man today. For the man of the house. Served him cake and coffee in bed.

Now we're sitting in our living room, which we painted, decorated, and filled with books and musical instruments. I'm trying to master the concertina that I was given as a birthday present; the scales are pentatonic and I feel as if the only way to learn them is to shut my eyes and just spin the melodies out into the air. I hope it doesn't take a toll on our cohabitation. We made a deal about letting the other person know if one of us is making too much noise.

Sometimes I bake apple cake; when you're out in the countryside, it's appropriate to use the oven as much as you can. I've never baked so much apple cake in such a short time. From a recipe of Grandma's. Otherwise, I'm trying these days to avoid yeast and sugar, because my left eardrum vibrates at the slightest rustle and someone said that it could be caused by an imbalance in my bacterial flora. We've gone out a few times to the little place on the corner and ordered flatcakes with sesame-seed bottoms and glasses of beer, but now we probably have to come up with some other sort of entertainment to break up the time and create weekends.

Our neighbor stopped by for coffee and warned us about the little swimming pool, how it was infected with a fungus, which had taken him a long time to clear from his toes. He actually said many other interesting things about life and bacterial growth. He invited my man to come with him some evening to one of the "man caves"; there were a few of them in this village and the neighboring ones. He said they had a special atmosphere: pool tables and wall calendars, vending machines filled with beer, easy chairs, and good stereos. You could chat about everything and nothing and be free and easy; be a teenager, free and easy.

My Birdy didn't take the invitation to visit a garage; I think he just forgot about it, or else hadn't wanted to become a teenager again. He was pretty thoughtful after the visit, and recalled a woman in her eighties he'd met at the sanatorium. She'd had fantastic purple nails and wore high-heeled, lace-up boots as she strutted down the hospital corridors and flirted with the *doc-o-tors*. The story went that she'd been a prostitute in her day, or at least kept the soldiers happy during the military occupation. She cleverly kept her home uncontaminated; never invited them into her living room, which was elegant, with perfectly embroidered pillows, and instead furnished her garage for this—in some people's opinions—very shameful alternate reality.

Aristotle said that someone who intended to contemplate knowledge and write could not live a family life; he would have to drag himself away from the city. The image of the hermit is a crippled old man who walks with a staff and a lantern out into the desert. Goes there alone to think, until he finds the answers to life's riddles.

Aristotle dwelt in contradictions, but was always trying to solve them, move towards the solution. But I think that the homes of philosophers—and perhaps others, as well—will always be contradictory.

Aristotle stated that thought had its home in complete quietude, far from the noise of the city, but said at the same time that a person could not develop into a moral being except in dialogue with others. That's perhaps how monasteries came into being, when those who fled the unrest for the desert discovered that they found it good to be with others, but only those who loved wisdom and respected their desire for quietude. The monastery provided a balance between being alone and engaging in conversation with others over glasses of wine made with grapes from its garden. The crying and laughter of children had no place there.

Those who didn't go all the way out into the desert, but still wanted to escape the children's racket, left their families from time to time, stepped through secret doors and became knights in the orders of brotherhood, puffing themselves up and sticking out their chests, adorned with the Order of the Falcon and other orders named after birds of prey.

I think that home shouldn't be a place you need to leave if you want to experience something in consonance with your innermost being. Home should be a place of experimentation and discovery, a place of peace and quiet where the most natural in each individual can be developed in fine-tuning to the desires and searches of others. A place of rest, as well. But yes, there is certainly something about the family home that doesn't quite work. And my notion of a different sort of family life is unclear.

I really want to find a kind of feminine solution within the whirlpool of our male-centered culture. There aren't so many women in history that you can look to for precedent. There are some, however. How was it with you, Persephone, the old Greek island goddess? Does the sound of your name hint at the frolicsome tranquility and revelation that we desire in our day? Can I trust my ears; is this a guiding sound, a leitmotif from the islands?

It sounds to me like deep down, Birdy's a family man, though he's understandably rebelling against family life, like most young men. Is it octagonal? he asked; this new family form, is it octagonal? I don't know, I said, maybe nonagonal . . . . The odd number is causing us some problems; we want the form to be provocative, yet protective. The family form is probably one that needs to be blown apart at regular intervals, to allow it to realign itself in the grass and grow from the soil anew.

I 'm able to get a lot of work done here. I find it best to work late into the night. I wake to my brother's knocking when he comes from town on official business in the countryside. I go down in my robe to open the door, then up to the kitchen to make buckwheat pancakes and coffee.

We have a couch in the kitchen, the old leather couch that Grandpa designed and had made. It's good to lie down after coffee and discuss the premises for the conservation of cultural heritage and other fundamental topics before he rushes off, no time to waste. Yet he often uses the opportunity to take a crap here first, which is the biggest vote of confidence in a home—if someone feels he has privacy enough for such a personal act in another's home, then it truly is a "privy place"—a "restroom," a place of repose.

My man enjoys these moments together too. He's usually finished with his work by then and ready to relax, and even more trust has developed between the two of them. They make fun of each other, which they actually did from the start, but always very congenially, and they regularly praise each other's outfits and comment on the fabric and weave. One says that Scottish woolens are best and the other says that Italian ones are better, and then they reminisce nostalgically on the woolens woven in Grandpa's workshop.

One day Birdy told my brother and me about a peculiar dream he'd had; well, he told me about it first, but I urged him to tell Owlie too. They both got very embarrassed and laughed loudly, but said nothing. Well, what the hell.

The dream went as follows: The ornithologist stuck his thumb deep into the cultural heritage manager's behind. Yes, as though it were perfectly natural, he said, laughing. And what then? I don't remember, said Birdy embarrassedly.

I made extra coffee, poured cups for them, and then filled a thermos for my brother. He always has a thermos with him, believes in thermoses, but I always forget to buy thermoses. But the word itself makes me as happy as a sprightly raisin bun shoving its way into the two-dimensional day.

Another visitor who stops by sometimes after his daily walk but doesn't use the privy is a wise squirrel, and he and Birdy talk about birds. Every day they see beautiful and rare birds, and once described one to me so enthusiastically: how it turned its hidden ear to the earth to listen for worms.

I probably go for walks at the wrong time, or am not quiet enough, as if I have a bell around my neck; I never see any rare birds, not even so much as a wren. But when I walk the old writers' streets, Bláskógar and Frumskógar, I often see a few gray-haired goldcrests going to the shop to buy popcorn and licorice during holidays. And pigeons on the square, probably from the old amusement park, ruffle-feathered and scruffy, the poor things, fed by the kindhearted shop queen.

It's strange to see the writers' houses turned into retirement homes. We searched for the foundation of the house that the poet Hannes and his wife Sunna had planned to build. They didn't get any further than that. Lived in temporary housing all their lives and had no children, but adopted a bird with a broken wing, which strutted around the house and defecated all over the living room. Which was a great vote of confidence. The poet then made the bird a staircase out of books, to make it easier for it to get to its water.

I've found three different trails and have made sure they don't cross private land, where territorial dogs might rush me. Sometimes I wander between the greenhouses that collapsed in the earthquake and look at the almost methodical arrangement of glass shards in the dirt. And my path leads to Laugaskarð. The colors there delight the eye: the turquoise swimming pool, pink and yellow balls, dark green conifers.

Sometimes we meet at the pool and are the only two there, swimming in snow or rain, the evergreen scent blending with the sulfury smell of the steam bath. He said that from the back, I looked like a little seal. I couldn't help but feel insulted, though I knew he meant well. To me, seals were devoid of feminine allure, and I felt as if he were suggesting to his pup to grow more hair, not more fat. But then I remembered Snorri the seal and kept on swimming, satisfied with the comparison. You're like an eider duck, I said, and he mentioned the first time his name appeared in print, in the magazine *Birds*, after he'd sent in a report about a stray migratory bird that he'd seen on the outskirts of town. But he mainly reminds me of a white falcon I saw painted on a wall in the Papal Palace in Avignon. Oh, maybe it's unlucky that he's a falcon if I'm a ptarmigan, he once said, which I really liked. So he's a ptarmigan cock, good-looking in both his winter and summer garb. Except that you're more like a tufted duck, the little brown one, he said; it's such a good diver.

We enjoy each other's company and I rarely feel as if I'm not having enough fun; it's more like we don't get enough of being alone, just the two of us. We've never talked so much in our lives—about anything and everything—but we also spend long, silent moments together, and laugh, too, and dance in the kitchen. We argue occasionally over formalities, and then there's a real uproar. It's kind of bad to end up arguing in the evening in this town; it's only happened once and I ran out but found nothing open, instead just walked in circles by the hot springs before going home, worried that he would be gone and I would be afraid of the dark, but when I got back he was just sitting in the kitchen, waiting calmly, with milk in an unbreakable glass. I was so glad to come home and we retired to our downy nest, rubbed our beaks together.

W e're on a trip to Reykjavík. I was teaching, and then
we visited some bookshops and had a nice time; are
going to stay at his mother's. I thought we would go less often;
it's surprising how frequently we find ourselves having to head
west over the heath. We're probably not self-sufficient enough
yet. But maybe it's also okay to make so many trips.

I definitely feel better being outside the city hub and going
in for things I think I want, apart from the necessities. We're
selective about the events we attend, and take our fine car, like
an old couple in fur hats and tails, to symphony orchestra concerts in the city, after reserving tickets well in advance. Brahms
and Bruckner, great applause.

Time together with friends is more festive, richer, in the
countryside than in the city. At least we always share good times
in our kitchen. When we sit and talk about the foundations of
culture and mental health, I feel good; it's never a waste of time.

The squirrel is very profound, and can turn into wolves and
plovers and all kinds of animals. He pets his cats, has a woman's
sensitivity and merges with the earth on his long walks; his
intelligence trickles in countless streams down through the turf,
allowing his mind to mature in the eternal cycles of nature, and
his feelings at the same time. And it's also great fun to see him

jump in and manhandle our boxes of books, give us a hand. And to hear about his old teenage passion for off-road motorcycles.

I took the car through an automatic car wash today. Felt claustrophobic and had to do Tibetan breathing to calm myself. But this also became a kind of healing.

Owning a car is a far more radical change than I could have imagined. My grandmothers said that they gained their greatest independence when they got their drivers' licenses and their first cars. And felt its loss most keenly when they could no longer drive; was this loss even more painful than losing their husbands?

Now I want even more worldly things: a dishwasher. An economical dishwasher, so that it would be easier to hold big dinner parties. Yes, you can get dragged into consumer society even while trying to keep it at a distance.

I t's really funny living in a place that isn't thought to have
much charm. There are no longer any monkeys in Eden,
and even though there are actually five libraries in the place,
and probably five swimming pools, people usually travel a bit
farther out of Reykjavík than here. Incredibly large numbers
of them, however, stop at the shop for ice cream.

I'm actually realizing now how incredibly conflicted I felt
in the big cities. I wanted by all means to offer lodging to
anyone who needed it, make them feel at home and enjoy every
moment with them. But then I would lose my workspace and
privacy.

Once I was complaining about it, but not really, because I
couldn't complain; I actually wanted things that way. But Mom
asked whether I couldn't find a cheap, nice guesthouse nearby
and send some of those people there. No, I didn't think I could.
But I knew she was right. She had experience; their home had
been like a café for years.

No one asks if they can stay with me here in Hveragerði.
And I can't complain about any real disturbances. Yet I can't
quite get into a rhythm. I decided to try to turn day into night.
Generally, I've found it best to write at night or in the Indian fire
hours between ten and two. My alternative therapist said that

if I continued like this, I would burn up all my bodily reserves, because during the fire hours one should rest.

I'm always trying to shut the world out when I work during the day; trying not to think about the bank and taxes and whether there's anything in the fridge to cook for dinner, if anything's going bad and needs to be used right away. But when the stores and the banks are closed, when even the tax director is sleeping, a velvety soft tranquility settles over everything. The only sounds are a pleasant buzz from the old refrigerator and snores from the throat of my male angel.

Yes, work's been going fairly well, and I generally reach perfect concentration and depth between ten and two. Then I let myself float slowly upwards and paddle around until morning, read a book and sleep until five. The only problem is that despite owing no one anything when I wake and getting work done, I still feel like a helpless pauper when I get up at such an ungodly late hour.

If the ornithologists and hikers are sitting in the kitchen when I wake, sipping tea, cawing and laughing, cracking nuts and racking their brains over something interesting, having finished their day's work, I feel like I'm stuck in a melancholy stupor, some heptagonal jumble, way behind schedule. Like all the migratory birds have gathered to leave—except for one who's still tending fledglings. People who are depressed, given to drink, or are socially handicapped all tend to be most active at night. Of course, Owlie is too, which I find comforting.

I've begun writing by hand on big scrolls of paper, like the Torah, in order to witness what I accomplish fill the room.

Otherwise, we never ever try to judge who's most productive; in fact it's quite clear that the squirrel would win such a contest. I'm trying to learn his working method. He seems, for example, to turn to translations when he wants to take a break from his own writing. It's instructive and rewarding to spend time with him, and we've done a lot of that this winter—he comes to us or we go over to his place, usually talk about literature and art, although the other day we watched a team-handball match together, and when the winter blues were on the verge of overwhelming us, we turned defense into offense and watched an old comedy that made us laugh uncontrollably for two hours.

We make reports to each other about books we've read or recently bought; we're all in the habit of adding more and more books to our middens, and it's nice to share our booty. And sometimes we argue; we aren't always in agreement about the excellence of certain authors, wonder why some of them are bad people, snooty and tiresome, yet good writers; we toss imaginary nuts at some of their heads if we're in that sort of mood.

This afternoon we're going to visit the farmers' market in Selfoss, and maybe stop at the Books and Coffee café. Have Indian food from the little food truck parked by the bridge over the Ölfus River.

My days are often pleasantly absurd here in the steam of the hot springs, but I can't quite capture them in words. Sometimes I stare out the window at the human life in this little village. The gait of the woman who regularly comes rambling through the snow and walks awkwardly into the shop is exactly how I feel these short, dark winter days. Last time I saw her, I called Birdy and asked him to come and check on me. He seemed almost angry, thought that I was belittling the woman or myself. Quite the contrary. I want to talk to her but rarely go down to the shop, nor do I know how I ought to go about it without bothering her. It's a routine that seemingly can't be broken: how she takes the same route back, her bag always full of popcorn. I wonder if she's buying it just for herself, or for everyone back at her retirement home?

I'm trying to carry myself in a more dignified manner on my daily walk, keep my back straight, hold my head high.

Should we go get some popcorn? I suggested. No, he didn't want to, but asked why I didn't just pop some myself when I felt like it; popcorn could hardly be called a meal. He was referring to a different conversation.

I complained about it the other day, or maybe didn't complain, but at least pointed out to him that he sometimes dropped completely out of us as a unit or unified household. As soon as I said it, I realized this was probably for the best, and that I should learn to adapt to his ways instead of trying to change him. Sometimes he'll just buy himself a sandwich for dinner and sit there munching on it, which flabbergasts me. What about our plans for dinner? Oh, did we have plans? he'll ask in surprise.

In return, he complained about how I complicated everything, never thought about dinner solely for me or for the two of us, always came up with ideas for inviting this or that person, maybe twelve people at the last minute, and then ended up stressed about how there might not be enough food.

I thought back on things and saw that there was a lot to what he said. At least, I can never think about dinner solely for myself unless I'm mad at him. Not even then. Then I use mealtime to smooth things over, ask if he's hungry. He's also quite right: when we decide to invite someone to dinner, I often take the opportunity to invite others, preferably the entire family. Make it really exciting. But then, after stirring up a storm of activity with my grand plans, I have the tendency, when the water is boiling and the oil is heating up, to pop into the storm's eye, because when I'm there, ideas can come pouring into my head. And in the meantime, everything burns . . .

You're always talking about peace and quiet, but as soon as you find it, you mess everything up, he said. He's pretty damned wise, and much more insightful than I dared to hope. We're trying to speak our minds, though it's difficult. More often,

I'm the one who goes for it, like a militant rat. I've got to be careful not to scratch out his eyes. I'm sometimes so quick to diagram the situation and identify the problem that his eyes cloud over and his head spins, he says. Then he tries to slow things down—whoa there, whirly bear!—and says that I jumble too many different things together. I've become absolutely convinced that this is the way problems have to be discussed sometimes: a problem is never an isolated thing—it goes hand in hand with other problems. Maybe in layers, strata—and you've got to go straight through them to get to the bottom of your problem.

I was just thinking about how we never actually hook up in bed anymore; he's asleep by the time I'm done working, and gets up long before I do. Sometimes I wake him by accident when I come to bed, startling him, though I try to be careful, but he says that I move like a cat, getting up so quickly when I think of something that I need to write down after I'm already in bed. He's sick and tired of it but tries not to show it, just wakes with a start wordlessly, like a wolf or fox. I try to slip calmly and quietly beneath the covers, sometimes do yoga exercises beforehand. But it's just so difficult to wean yourself off of instinctual reactions and move slower, particularly when ideas come so quickly, rushing up in waves from the deep.

From a sexual point of view, it's better to be compared to a cat than a seal, I think. But this discrepancy in our waking hours can certainly become a hindrance to sex.

I asked him whether we should meet regularly in our bedroom in the middle of the day. Yes, we certainly should, he said. Showed up just as the clock struck three, ears perked, only I'd lost track of time and was sitting there in my shabby bathrobe with bird's-nest hair and sleep in my eyes, trying to create a crossword puzzle. We decided just to play chess instead; he's teaching me how the pieces move. He's a patient teacher and sometimes lets me win. But I haven't completely connected yet with my inner chess master. Panic is my weakness. And when I panic, I can't concentrate on the game; I start thinking about chess as a phenomenon, which is probably some sort of defense mechanism. Whether the rook could be called Puck, or whether that name might be better for the bishop, who actually has a cloven head, like a jester.

I've been contemplating desperate measures. Whether it might be a good idea to plan for some "arousal time," rent soft-porn movies down at the shop and go buy garter belts from the clothing and fabric store. The notorious quagland erotic. Shame that I could never do a striptease for him; I'm sure I'd start laughing. Has our relationship become a brother-sisterly one? Where the laughter and warmth of closeness take up so much space that there's none left for sexual desire?

Maybe, for us, a door is opening to the carnival, where lust becomes laughable and laughter lusty. Will burlesque be our next experiment, then? Or is that like porn: a terminus, a predictable parody of desires for those who haven't dealt with the humiliation of lust for power or powerlessness? Porn is about shame, but it never opens into humility; it corners desire, never allowing it to transform. The repeat indulgence stunts development. Still, some people do seem able to nourish themselves curiously well, even aesthetically, on porn, yet I've never met anyone who's developed just as well from it emotionally.

I remember how terribly disappointed I was with porn as a breakthrough in Western sexual attitudes. Is this the whole transgression, then? Will it never be any more original than this? No, I don't mean uglier, more exaggerated, but rather, more introspective, more psychologically provocative, without becoming violent? Isn't it more exciting to test the limits of cohabitation without short-circuiting into violence?

In porn no one listens, either to themselves or to others. I tried, for example, to explain to an old dog that it would be nice to be bitten on the back of the neck, like how a bitch bites its puppies—so much affection in the drool. Then he went and got a black dress that he said was made of the same material as a dog's nose and asked me to put it on. I found it funny to be turned into a rubber nose. But our fantasies were completely at odds. He went and got a rope, hoping to tie the puppy up and beat it.

How naïve I can be; such a giant half-wit. Aw, I don't feel like telling the rest. Luckily, I remembered that dogs have claws, and got myself out of that brutal burlesque.

Left him there on stage, with the props of his fantasies. Poignant solitude. He who was so happy to have finally found his equal in perversity. The key that opened that world of desire was a dog's wet nose. Yet it would probably have been useless to try to explain that, even if our worlds were parallel, they had nothing in common except the nose. He wouldn't have listened.

I tend to think that women are aroused by other types of breakthroughs. That a man's fantasies are bound to the system; in their world, the carnival is seen through the eyes of the king—where people get the chance to be king for a day, where everyone changes roles, but then it all goes back to normal again. People slink home after their trip to the theater. With their tails between their legs. The secretary who became a sex-bomb turns back into a secretary, the doctor who became a rapist turns back into a doctor. Just a bit too predictable. And just a bit too close to the standardized, unspeaking violence.

It's important to avoid all standardization in sex. Set out on your own research expedition into the jungle of personal, animalistic urges and allow them to find an outlet in the web of highly-developed love. If you simply pursue your urges, you immediately wind up in Freudian standards that capitalism has adopted, and that literature uses to sell itself. But if you follow your urges into the unknown dimensions of love, something exciting and beautiful is bound to happen.

Well, enough theorizing. I'm lying in bed and the stack of books on the floor next to me is so tall now that I could climb out the window without touching the floor.

O ur house is a mess. Handwritten scrolls—each containing a different chapter of my book—litter the floor of my room, the kitchen, and the living room. I tiptoe through the chapters to get a grasp of the structure. I would normally never allow such a takeover of my space unless I were alone and under terrible time constraints. Birdy is tolerant, but had grown anxious by the fourth day and, without a word, fled to the peace and quiet of the library, finding my ultra-precise system of chapter divisions, all over the floor, to be utter chaos. I'm trying to be sassy, carefree. Make a mental promise to him and to me to tidy everything up again as soon as I've submitted.

Although my final deadline has passed, I've got to pretend now as if I have enough time, eat a piece of toast with pâté, even read an old paper. Fortunately, he's not here stressing out about me missing my deadline. You can't accomplish anything with a worrywart around.

The other day he was supposed to submit a report to the research fund, to convince the high council that his bird book was a necessary contribution to Iceland's literary fauna. I felt as if I couldn't do my work in the meantime, as if it would interfere with his report-writing. As long as I slept, I thought, and especially if I dreamed of birds, or if I got ready for work calmly and quietly and made everything cozy at home, his writing would go well. I brought him tea and kissed him on the neck, wordlessly, and then over lunch we talked about the different tones of reports; I just fixed up something simple, without any fuss. But as soon as I sat down at my desk and started working at full steam, he got up and said he was going to the library; he couldn't concentrate anymore.

Can't we both concentrate fully on work at the same time? Does one of us have to be on household duty, to maintain the balance? Like when you have young children—you can't really focus on your computer or a book, even if they're totally wrapped up in playing. It seems you have to either take part in the game or just be there, just be. A gentle, ubiquitous presence. Your concentration mustn't be exclusive.

When I think back on it, I realize that up until now, I never managed to concentrate fully on my work while living with a man. If I needed to finish a project, I had to leave, be somewhere completely alone. Or with Mom. Both of us can focus and work hard at the same time, singing as we do so and then treating ourselves afterward. I've experienced similar moments with friends, but too damned rarely with men that I've lived with. And now the big question is whether I can get any quiet time for myself from the man I've chosen to live with.

He's been so good to me the last few days, cooking and doing the dishes with housewifely charm. He's been on phone and social duty, keeping in touch with family and friends so as not to lose the thread, to keep the wool spinning. That's usually my job, and it feels good to let go. Still, the other day I asked, just to be sure, whether he'd spoken to his sister about her birthday party next weekend. He asked me to try not to think about the party until it's time, and absolutely not to think about a gift.

After I submit, I'm going to air out the duvets and pillows, put on a checkered dress and makeup, throw a tablecloth on the table, cook us a delicious stew, swimming with mushrooms, and then open a bottle full of fermented berries. Maybe offer a mix-in for dessert—ice cream with smashed-up Smarties is a customer favorite at the shop. The grinder is quite noisy; my eardrums quiver.

We saw a house advertised for rent in Eyrarbakki and drove out there this morning. Are we fleeing ourselves? I asked. Will we always find faults with our accommodations because of the turmoil in our own hearts? He pushed the jalopy to the limit. Held onto the gear stick with a veiny, thin hand. Asked me to switch songs just a bit less frequently; I was in charge of the music and was constantly trying to find the perfect song for our trip, going from one to the next; yes, of course, such a thing can get tiring. His family is from here in the wetlands.

Finally I found a song to match his driving, taking into account the landscape, the weather, the time, our mood: *Rey a quien reyes adoran. The king whom the kings adore*—or whom women adore? A wild tambourine revel from the sixteenth century.

We raced through moss-covered mountains toward the sea, until the sand dunes and salty waves welcomed us. He showed me the house that his great-great-grandfather built. And the houses with Samúel roofs—compare them with Gröndal's salt-box. Were your grandpa and grandma happy here? I asked. Yes, as far as I know, he said, and recently a wise woman slipped me some documents about them, including the funeral poem that he wrote about Grandma. Longing, pure and simple. When he said this, I wanted immediately to move with him to Eyrarbakki, especially since I've always liked it there.

The rental house is weather-sealed but unfinished, with a yard, where we saw an upside-down tricycle and plastic shovels and buckets strewn about. Peculiarly bleak. Is this maybe like our dream, upside-down? It's like I can sense the depression of those who flee the city for nature, but who end up shut inside their own shells and never even go for walks on the beach, he said. Maybe we'll always be on the run. No, no, we'll find a place to be.

We took a look at the house and I was excited to sign a lease; I thought the yard offered a lot of possibilities, and it would be fun to live near a cemetery. We went for a walk and I convinced my saint that this was our future. But then it turned out that the lease was only four months, and that a cat came with the house. What if we have to go somewhere unexpectedly?

There were four dead ravens on the beach, and on the way back I put a sorrowful old song on the player: *The king is dead*, with the same Joculatorium band as before. The sea will probably draw us back to it later.

We do little more than peruse real-estate websites. It's tiring, paying mental visits to so many houses, arranging our books against so many different walls, trying to piece together where they'll all fit. Imagining the atmosphere. Which I do while listening to music and wiggling my toes.

He fell asleep happy and beautiful and I slipped as quietly as I could out of bed and went and sat in front of the computer. *The Profound Desire of the Gods*. A very beautiful movie about life on an island in Japan where mothers and daughters are close and siblings have children. The leading actress really reminds me of Puck, that spry old jester. Laughter from the bowels of the earth. By the end of the movie, everyone's planning to sell the island to the Chinese, but the brother, whom everyone thinks is crazy because he loves his sister, is the only one who refuses to sell.

It was with a sense of nostalgia that I said goodbye to Hveragerði and made the move over Kambar, looking back to see the glowing greenhouses, although I must admit that it surprised me not to be able to buy fresh vegetables at this nursery center. Eden burned to ashes. Adam and Eve, carved in oak, escaped unharmed. Just barely. And then there's the pollution from the power plant hanging over the village.

My uncle Hare came to visit and told us, out of the blue, that the apartment was infested with a so-called house-mold; he'd been fighting against the same thing for a long time and recognized its appearance and smell. He had a look around and said that since the electricity was highly unstable, the noxious stuff just went on a rampage. He advised us to get out of there before we lost our hair or our minds and our immune systems crumbled. Birdy was always coming down with the flu.

We put all of our stuff in storage. We don't know where we're going next. My man is staying at his great-grandpa and grandma's summer cottage for a while. He called me and said that he'd finally cleared out his old storage space in Reykjavík, thrown out a bunch of junk and put the rest in our new storage unit. He sounded relieved; his voice brighter than before. And remarkably enough, in his next breath he said that he'd gone to his father's for lunch and had a very good, sincere chat about issues that aren't normally on the table. As if he'd gotten rid of some clogs while clearing out his stuff. He's reading the *Saga of Þórður Geirmundarson* by Benedikt Gröndal. I miss him and want to hear his laugh, remember when he started reading that comic story, lying on our blue-green Ottoman bed and laughing out loud, wholeheartedly.

I have two boxes of books with me, clothes, shoes, and cosmetics, and plan on staying at my brother's place for a while. Hopefully the mold won't follow me. I've begun dreaming a lot again, mainly about antiquities. It's clearly the influence of my brother the relics-man. It's so exciting when he comes home from his day trips, steps out of the Land Rover in his cowboy boots and tells you, for example, that he thinks he's found an old grave mound. Question is whether it's the same grave mound that Kristján Eldjárn dug up back in the day; we'll see, he says meaningfully. Pagan graves are so rarely found in Iceland. The glacial river has taken a new course, making it possible to get to it. He's applied for all the necessary permits and hopes to be able to start digging shortly. I can go with him as an amateur, and slink around for relics. But he's got to have a specialist in human bones with him, as well as other experts. Yes, and a good shovel!

After dinner, he took a little box out of the freezer and opened it, showed me a tiny bronze bell found in an excavation up north and that was now on its way to be studied.

I occasionally pop over to the museum, where there's always something interesting to see. Yesterday I noticed the colors in the old conjoined house, which is built partly of turf and partly of timber. The guest room is a light royal blue, like the houses in Mexico, the hallway is turquoise, the writing desk dark green, the small organ reddish-brown, the kitchen creamy yellow, and the side room trout pink. Today I had a look at ear picks made of silver and pictures that I have no idea how I missed: a series of framed, embroidered names of the different spaces in the old farmhouse: *family room and kitchen, pantry, living room, upstairs family room, dining room, storehouse, barn, manure shed, drying shed, passage, smithy, stable, dung shed, barn, passage, main door, weighing house, storage room, attic, extension* . . . then I found plans of farmhouses and descriptions of landscape, farms, and their inhabitants by a woman whose district is so dear to her, Helga Skúladóttir. She writes about Keldur in the Rangárvellir district and other old farmsteads in the hope of putting them into context within global cultural history, and states, in the preface to her book: *Iceland's farms shall now be able to connect with each other by means of spiritual bonds, just as its cultural center, our city of Reykjavík, could connect with the major cultural institutes of the world* . . .

I'm sitting here with a report on an excavation and feel like an apprentice—an excitable, restless disciple who is spoon-fed culture like a patient is fed grapes. I'm happy that my little brother knows the ins and outs of all of this, he's the master, but I can enjoy the poesy in the reports and learn new words. *Albarello* is a jar for holding ointment.

I see here, in this hugely entertaining report, that among other things, seven bronze pieces were found in the excavation; it's uncertain what their purpose was, or if they're pieces of something, but I think they could have been part of a percussion instrument. Just let me make a wild guess. Also found in this excavation were several opals, turquoise stones, and fragments of jasper, which may have been used to start fires, along with grindstones and churns. The barn was full of hay leavings.

Owlie is still outside inspecting things, but I was so cold that I crawled into the car. We're out on a heath close to the road and at first there was little to see, a slight elevation of the ground but few signs of the great farm that stood here in olden times. It was buried completely under a blanket of ash in 1362, when Öræfajökull Glacier erupted and the settlement was deserted. Several decades ago, the site was excavated, revealing a building that was neither a Viking longhouse nor a passage-farmhouse, but something else, or a combination of both, and that's now considered indicative of an entire, little-understood time period. I immediately got excited that this mystery period in the history of Icelandic architecture might be a mystery in other areas, as well, and that, with more thorough excavation, something new might be discovered about the Icelandic national spirit, something upon which to build. But what's the difference between a Viking longhouse and a passage-farmhouse? As far as I can tell, the two styles represent a development from a single, shared space into a number of different "compartments" connected by a single passageway. Did the passageway cease to be a humble link and expand into a central component? Gable farms then developed from passage-farms, the central passageway dark and cramped. Some clever person out west sketched a gable farm and the sketch made the rounds, and today we can still walk around such farms. But we don't know the actual size of the farm here in Gröf; we don't know how the spaces were connected. All we really know is that the farm is a combination of two architectural styles of the past and future, from the North and the South. What's more, there are two things that seem to me to be special about this dwelling, judging by the report: on the one hand, the "bathroom," and on the other, the kiln house.

As strange as it is to drive around Álftafjörður and see all the swans, it's fun to hear that in the bathroom on this farm, people actually did bathe themselves. According to the report, it's likely that in this central space of the house there was a sauna, as was common in Greenland. And that birch was probably burned on rocks, which would have been invigorating and therapeutic. I sensed the truth of this arrangement; naturally, the heart of the house, its center and main space, should be a place of refreshment and regeneration, a cleansing and healing room. Presumably, issues were discussed there as they are in the public hot tubs today, as openly as pores dripping with sweat.

Perhaps in those days, the power of conversation among all the members of the household was greater than it is today. It seems to me as if later, in family rooms and parlors, one particular person was responsible for imparting wisdom, while the others simply listened—work and the mouth were no longer connected. Bible readings and the radio aren't very conducive to conversation and questions.

I have difficulty imagining how it all looked, despite the realistic descriptions of the kiln and storehouse, octagonal ash containers, pantry and bathroom, double adjoined cowshed, etc. The archaeologists are trained to imagine the connections.

What type of farm stood here? Presumably, the people here were entirely self-sustaining, while simultaneously in diverse and complex relationships with the environment and others in the region and the world. It was a short distance to the sea and harbors.

We took great liberties trying to fill in the gaps. Then we called Mom and described the ruins to her, because she's so good at visualizing things from descriptions. We asked her to envision the house. Strode over the heath and he found the place where the kiln house presumably stood. It was Orcadian in shape, he said. And although I didn't understand at all how he came to that conclusion, I thought it was the best news I'd heard in ages. What's that? Orcadian in shape? Well, what the hell? The historians had better watch out! A kiln house of unusual make, previously unknown in Iceland. Maybe like a towering silo, where grain for grinding was dried. Barley, too, and stinging nettles. Perhaps aromatic herbs as well? And medicinal herbs? But what word is this, actually; "*sofn*"? Oh, of Irish origin, of course. Like Icelandic women?

I felt homesick standing there on the gravel bank. There must be some Irish tradition that bears remembering now that we're standing at a crossroads in Iceland. An Irish tradition, every sort of tradition.

Could it be that people didn't want to acknowledge their Irish heritage since it was connected to women and slaves?

But if we want to reconstruct some sort of aristocratic, "chieftain" culture where people stand steadfast in their respect for themselves as well as others, shouldn't we then acknowledge the slaves in us? So that we can humbly come to understand our responsibility to serve nature and each other? Might this Irish heritage be one of the things that slumbers in the lowest strata of our consciousnesses, and even beneath the waters of our subconsciousnesses?

Yes, yes, the cultural heritage manager is prepared for this debate. But he warns me not to be blinded by the Celtic cross. Told me about scholarly prejudices against amateur enthusiasts who have a burning interest in everything that the scholars don't talk enough about. One of those is the settlement of Iceland before the settlement and continuous Celtic influence, from the time of the *papar* colony. Since the sources are often limited, it's occasionally necessary to refer to unconventional evidence such as stone crosses and astronomy. And although there are often really interesting connections, ones that were certainly underestimated, it sometimes seems as if they're made via a short circuit over to a kind of religious conviction. Then it's as if people abandon dialogue and are convinced in their solitude of some unified framework that turns out to be too difficult to communicate to others. The proliferation of scholarship and dialogue needs to be promoted to the periphery. Unfortunately, these theories and these hidden and unified visions have been shoved off the table in academia, perhaps due to arrogance or perfectly understandable fear of charlatanry, insanity, and popularism.

Before we return home, he's going to do a quick sketch of the ruins, because he says that you connect to a site when you sketch it yourself, and better recollect your musings on a site's significance when viewing your own drawings.

I recall him telling me that some people smiled indulgently when he submitted his first reports, because they were full of romantic descriptions of the vegetation, and beautiful little blossoms drawn on and around the ruins.

I was making oatmeal and imagining how it would be to put my hand into the ground and reach down through the ages, when the cultural heritage manager returned from his research expedition and told me that he'd stuffed his hand into a hole in the grave mound and pulled out a dead bird. What bird was it? He didn't know; it was totally decomposed. He said it still gave him the creeps. Due to your fear of birds? I asked. No, no. But two archaeologists died just after discovering this grave, before they were able to examine it in detail. Then I also felt creeped out and frightened; I've always been afraid of my loved ones dying prematurely, particularly him.

He offered to take me for a drive after lunch. He needed to check whether there were any ruins on a plot of land that some summer-cottage owners were going to start developing. What a plague these cottages are, all throughout the country. Entire farms bought and turned into summer-cottage developments. Regional awareness is entirely lacking in these developments, or better yet, undevelopments. There are no connections to the earth. At least it seems that way when you drive around such places in a jacked-up SUV.

You might say, however, if I'm to jabber a bit more to myself, that this new settlement on the grounds of love of nature, delight in solitude, and often, nostalgia for the old days in the countryside or the rural telephone network . . . bridges gaps and is positive. No, no, no problem. It's just bad when ownership of the earth is transferred into even fewer hands than before, to private concerns that only think about renting or selling as many parcels as they can.

People from town view the land beneath summer cottages as plots, not as the earth. An integrated vision of the land has been lost. Our relationship with nature needs to be renewed, our connection to the future. In this prolonged limbo and uncertainty, we're lacking a vision of the future. And I'm talking about Iceland as a whole. And about myself as part of the whole . . .

M y room is adjacent to the master bedroom and faces the house where none other than the curator lives, with his sister and her husband. She's intelligent and good-looking, like a rare bird. She grows roses and knits insoles with island-patterns.

A few months ago I dreamed that I lived in the same house as the curator and shopped at the same fish shop, where fresh fish was always on offer, a pile of char fillets, and the fishmonger asked if I was like my neighbor, who ate only char fillets, and I said yes, that was the case. I don't know what the dream meant; maybe it will become clear. It was so big, that pile of char, massive, reached up over the display case.

Yesterday I walked up to the woods and saw an owl. Walked back as if in a trance, staring between the trees and feeling a delicate, childish joy seep through me. Happy that it didn't frighten me. Nor was it cruel-looking at all, just fluttered silently above me and allowed me to look.

I looked forward to telling Owlie the news, because he shares my obsession with owls. We recalled when we saw the swan come flying toward the igloo we'd built and land in front of it. We thought it was a prehistoric bird, having never seen a swan so close. We called Grandma on the rural phone to tell her that we'd seen some kind of ostrich down by the river and heard giggling on the line; whoever was eavesdropping couldn't restrain themselves. But now he told me that I probably hadn't seen a snowy owl—they were so enormous—he wondered whether it might have been a short-eared owl, instead. Apparently they're white on the chest and under the wings.

I called Birdy and told him the news, too. I felt like I'd been touched by something divine, the essence of nature, its innermost sound. To get to see it for real, and so close, after having seen it so often in dreams. Like seeing the boundaries between dreams and waking, in the flesh. I was still unconvinced that it wasn't a snowy owl, and he said that they looked like headless swans. No, then it was a short-eared owl, I said, and he said that it was a very good thing to see a short-eared owl, very good for me. We're planning to meet halfway at summer solstice. Find ourselves a cave. Maybe the *Paradise Cave*; I feel a tingle when I think of Jón Trausti's novel.

My brother and I cooked beef tongue with tarragon, chatting all the while. Immersed ourselves in one of those conversations that seem bottomless, like a great revelation, bringing deeper understanding and joy that you feel in your bones. After chatting a bit about the cohabitation model, we agreed that the old extended-family household was the future, if we could find it a new form.

Yet I do have a few reservations about the extended-family phenomenon. I've been recalling Hannah Arendt's definition of public space and its extinction, of the origins of totalitarianism and the end of democracy. I've often found myself thinking of her ideas when I visit other people's homes. It's as if the shared

spaces are passive in some way, spaces where it's possible to
relax and think in close proximity to your nearest and dearest
and develop fellowship, overcome difficulties. Yet sometimes
attempts are made to create shared space that teenagers flee,
escaping to their rooms, well equipped with the latest gadgets.

It sounds clichéd to say it, but maybe television has taken
over our shared space. Or the anxiety that the shared space isn't
fun enough. That stress then infects our vacations, when the
car trip becomes unbearable from the get-go, and the teenagers would rather jump out because they're so used to just going
to their rooms and not needing to contribute anything to the
whole. Some continue to be teenagers and never realize that
they bear just as much responsibility for the atmosphere as
the others. Then there are others who presume to bear more
responsibility than anyone else. The golden mean isn't easily
navigated in a packed family car!

When I asked my grandma up north about a woman's space,
she replied that the cowshed was probably best. The greatest
peace and quiet was to be found there. Thinking in proximity
to animals is completely different than thinking alone.

Hannah Arendt said that everyone needed to have his or
her own space, where he or she was in control, but that people
needed to have access to other space, shared space, median
space, or what she called the public space, which no one con-
trols. Where there's enough space to discuss issues both seriously and jokingly. Where they can share their experience, their
own stories and also their visions for the future.

People have criticized Arendt as a romantic fool who didn't
see that people never step into this public space except to try to

gain control over it and persuade others of their own opinions and interests. Yes, that's how politics are and have been most of the time. Arendt looked back and saw intolerance of the public forum that has no predetermined agenda. And intolerance of space that is not under the control of something specific.

Arendt described totalitarianism as a centuries-old tendency to expand the private space into an all-pervasive common forum that is in fact not a space of freedom but an illusion, this expansion leaving people with neither quietude in private nor space for free, unrestrained deliberation in a real public space. But as the earth calls for biodiversity, democracy calls for respect for the diverse voices within the community, which again calls for a public space that is made of what matters the most: true interest between different individuals at different times.

H e's frying flatbread with a welding torch, which is a rather messy procedure. His moon-cakes are good with butter, even when burned. It's midnight and we're idling away, each of us singing our own song, I noticed. Just like back at home in the old days, everyone singing his own song, often the same songs again and again. We were also reminiscing on some space-items at home. The so-called "Interval" was a great solution, where the smoked lamb and ptarmigan were hung up. Dad put radios in all the rooms, so that when you turned one off, whatever program was on could still be heard throughout the house. And Mom held meetings in the bathroom; she'd really liked Stöng, where old Gaukur lived—and it was there that fundamental issues were discussed, in an excellent state of grounding.

We talked about our trips to Istanbul, where we'd gone this winter, two weeks apart, though it would have been better if we'd gone together. He regretted not having seen the runic inscriptions in the Hagia Sophia: *I was here*. Gaukur from Stöng is also thought to have inscribed his name and a similar message on a rock in Orkney. But the nice buildings there in old Byzantium are somewhat blurred in my memory. I remember having a good time in the Blue Mosque, thought of something very important there but don't remember what it was; wrote it down, but in what notebook, I don't know. While there I had a passion for roses and the color blue, and was completely enthralled by the Mosque of Blue Roses. Came out of it with an Indian writer and we bought a warm-milk and lotus drink spiced with cinnamon and had a look at statues of holy men that appeared more akin to teddy bears and discussed doctoral dissertations that grow so long they take revenge on novels. Also discussed literary diversity in the spirit of biodiversity. How can we nurture marginal forms in literature? Then I saw a wall covered with ivy, which probably inspired my passion for it, taking over from my rose-passion. I wondered how the strands crawled up along the continent, across all borders, over the bullet wounds on buildings and the ax scars on trees.

Birdy called and asked whether my brother and I were still jabbering. You two sure do like to jabber, he said amicably. He announced that he was on his way to Istanbul, where he'd been invited to a bird conference. Well, what a coincidence, we were just talking about Istanbul! I'll just manage to say goodbye to him before he leaves. His body is still in me after our stay in a cave; we broke into an old *papar* cave in the Landsveit area and saw seven crosses when we lit a candle, inched our way farther and farther in with a bottle of port, aromatic oils, and a down pillow. Completely unauthorized. The locals and cultural heritage managers never knew.

Owlie is outside building a frame for the composter, having planted a vegetable garden and dreaming of an orchard. Lying here in the privy is the book *Pagan Graves and Grave Goods*, which I look through when I get the chance. It occurred to me to apply for a job at the museum, and I ran the idea by Owlie.

Then I could maybe get an apartment here in the countryside right nearby and live with my man, and he could conduct his bird research here, where there are plenty of birds in the woods. Owlie, however, said he thought it might be an unrealistic plan; I was far too much of a wanderer to be able to commit myself to such work. But I want to stop wandering, I said, and asked him to call and check whether they needed anybody at the museum. He looked at me and asked with wise eyes whether that was really what I wanted.

The ivy twisting round the oaks like bristled serpents. The day
cold—a warm shelter in the hollies, capriciously bearing berries . . .

DOROTHY WORDSWORTH
ALFOXDEN JOURNAL

I got out of the bus at the wrong stop and walked a long way without knowing where I was, listening with delight to the bleating of the sheep. I was raised thinking that the word "bleating" was in the neuter gender, but the other day I heard someone use it in the masculine, and find the change amusing; maybe I could even put it in the feminine. In any case, the sheep here are strange—their wool cut close and their flesh firm; the lambs are like fuzzy fish dumplings.

I drifted with the wind into the church, which was full of hay; the fragrance was wonderful, but no one was there. I saw St. Oswald, who was said to have trained himself in prayer and elevated himself above the weaknesses of the flesh, and lying throughout the church were embroidered hassocks with images of all sorts of natural phenomena: ice and snow, lightning, umbilical cords, and animals. A little sign stated that William had planted yew trees and daffodils in the churchyard with the help of his sister Dorothy, in remembrance of the children who had died and the children who were never born.

I went into the churchyard and saw the graves of these siblings and the dark green trees. I think that they were the most beautiful trees I'd ever seen. I didn't have a pen with me and repeated the name so as not to forget it: *yew tree, yew tree, yew tree*. Continued on and into Grasmere village, where proudly sauntering jackdaws welcomed me, and I said *hi ho* and knew that I was back on track. And yes, indeed, it was the village of the two siblings.

I was on cloud nine, having arrived at the roots of Romanticism. So it was a shock to walk around the village, peek into the shop windows and see all the pillows embroidered with rotten daffodils and various other things related to the story of the Lake District poets. It's one thing to remember, another to get stuck. Why don't people buy notepads and write poems instead of sit around on historical poem-pillows watching TV? Why not renew Romanticism, re-clarify the relationship between creation and memory?

Well, I myself have come here pretty much like a dog, sniffing out monuments. Excited about the memorabilia: the locks of hair that the poet sent with his letters, the candles that he himself made from sheep tallow and used for writing. He hadn't wanted to write at a regular desk, but instead used a lap desk, which I had a good long look at, among other things. Maybe it's just a question of aesthetics. If we cross some indefinable and subtle line in the reconstruction and exaltation of the past, we feel as if aesthetics and beauty are stagnating, which must be a contradiction in itself—stagnant beauty, standardized beauty. Surely beauty must be in motion. Or be motion.

My guidebook on this trip of mine is the journal of Dorothy Wordsworth, the sister of the famous Romantic poet William Wordsworth. I came across this book on the electric stage and fell into it. It's incredibly exciting, even though it's not really about anything. And yet, it's about so much. For example, you get to know whether her brother slept well or badly on this or that day, whether he sat writing late into the night or not. After reading it, I felt I had to come here and see the siblings' house, find out about their life together, discover whether the dwelling they shared might reveal something of the closeness of their relationship. If I could learn from it.

I'm going to find Dove Cottage. Dorothy describes the great amount of time she spent with her brother in the orchard there, where they lived together after having been orphaned and separated for many years. In this orchard, William rewrote his poems and she read them over and emended them, and then wrote in her diary or perhaps composed some poems of her own, which haven't survived. Sometimes he laid his hand on her shoulder as she read. As she describes it, and judging by his poems, the trust between them was perfect.

They walked in the evenings on paths solely their own; they alone knew the paths leading to a little mossy cave or earthen bower far up on the hill above Dove Cottage. There they sat and chatted and looked out over the lakes. I'm in Lakeland.

I hadn't reserved a hotel room, couldn't figure out from the map how everything was situated. I walked farther and farther toward the lakes, in the direction of the mountains, as the bleating grew louder in my ears, but there were no rooms available. I'd started feeling a bit desperate late last evening and ended up accepting a last-minute offer for accommodation in the most expensive hotel I've ever been in. I'm sitting now in a pink, plush-parlor, surrounded exclusively by old people.

I decided to enjoy my room to the fullest and ran the bath, poured myself a glass of Grouse whisky and wrote several letters on the special hotel stationery.

Hanging on the wall above the bed is a poor reprint of Van Gogh's sunflowers, making me think of our courtship in the painter's old haunts, when we watched the movie about him and were so upset by that bastard Gauguin, whom Van Gogh had invited to join him and paint in the peace and quiet of the south, and had prepared for the coming of this friend of his by painting sunflowers in every room in the house. He was so excited to see his friend, who turned out to be a real asshole.

The breakfast menu was very aristocratic and rustic, as if the hotel's main clientele were landed gentry; the breakfast room reminded me of the old farmer hotels at Lake Mývatn, where

British birdwatchers would sit alone at their tables, browsing articles on the behavior of harlequin ducks.

I read somewhere that Wordsworth and his sister had always had so-called *porridge* for breakfast, and there it was on the menu, so I ordered it and asked the waiter what it was. He said that it was, in fact, an indescribable phenomenon, which made me terribly excited to try it. Would you like anything else? he asked, and I ordered a sausage just to be on the safe side. Then was ceremoniously brought a bowl of oatmeal on a tray. Admittedly, it was exceptionally good oatmeal, served with cream, it seemed—a good start to the day, in any case. After I'd completely cleared my rosy bowl of oatmeal, my sausage came sailing in on a silver platter.

A fter browsing a bit in the little bookshop in the village and mailing my letters, I went to Dove Cottage. First I visited a special exhibition at the museum next door, about the ever-writing Shelleys and the small, smeared book clump that turned out to be the "Journal of Sorrow" that Mary Shelley, the monster-mother, wrote after her husband died; the book had landed in the water. And I also saw several beautiful things that belonged to Coleridge, who was a close friend of Dorothy and William.

On display in a plush-lined glass cabinet was William's wedding ring, and next to it were long psychological reports on his sister's eccentricities. There was a reference to her journal entry on her brother's wedding day. She wrote that he'd asked her to sleep with the ring on the eve of the wedding, and that when she gave him the ring, they'd embraced as if in parting. Afterward, she'd thrown herself onto her bed and wept.

Naturally, she was happy for her brother to be marrying that good woman; she loved their children as her own and made them a little playroom, lined its walls with newspapers and created a fantastic space. It was natural to weep at such a celebratory moment, in pure compassion and joy. What's more, Dorothy had no one else to turn to. She and Coleridge were friends and shared an opium addiction, but she never had her own family. He, on the other hand, had a family, but never managed to overcome the adolescent inside him, and his family was divided and hurt and he ended up living with a friend, with his pipe, ink, and the intoxicating oil.

I was in a festive mood as I entered Dove Cottage, but after making my way through it and stepping out the back door and into their orchard, I became reverential; time stopped for a moment.

It was so beautiful that I could barely breathe. The first thing that greeted me was the blessed ivy, which enwraps the buildings and trees, the walls and bridges, breaches of trust and wounded hearts.

I'm sitting in the mossy cave where the siblings spent many hours, looking out over the countryside and writing poems. Their friend Coleridge often came along. Dorothy describes his trip up to the cave: *We saw him climbing up towards a rock. He called us, and we found him in a bower—the sweetest that was ever seen. The rock on one side is very high, and all covered with ivy, which hung loosely about, and bore bunches of brown berries.*

And there's the wood cranesbill and the pink bells that are called thimble-blossoms in Icelandic, and which adorn the garden in Skógar as well.

I left the orchard at noon; the sun shone brightly and bees were buzzing. I wanted to stay longer; the rowan trees formed a frame, as in my cultural heritage manager's yard back home. The other day, we sat on a wooden bench in the grove and talked about the countryside; he brought up the old sheep sheds that had burned down—he'd always felt best there, when we had the night shift during lambing. Those were our best times together, when we felt mild pangs of nostalgia for Dad and Mom; we had to stand tall, together, and discovered that we could rely on each other.

I walked through the forest, taking the same path as the two siblings of old, conversing in deepest understanding. The loud bleating of brothers and sisters, separated from their mothers in milking pens. I went a bit farther and over onto another path to get to the next house, where the entire family moved after having lived in Dove Cottage for eight years. Big, fat red squirrels vaulted on their tails between the trees. I peed in the forest and ate raspberries. I was feeling sensitive and poetic; gazed at the lakes, walked backwards. The bag on my back was heavy, holding the complete works of Wordsworth and *Lyrical Ballads*.

At the next museum, the home of Wordsworth, his wife, and sister for many years, all the Romantic in me had disappeared. I tried to show interest in the house, consider the arrangement of space with scientific precision; yes, there the poet finally had his own workroom, above his sister's bedroom. With a view of the lakes. And there was a library, to some degree. But the spirit was gone. It was either not in the house, or not in me. As when mammals no longer give milk, not a drop, even when the best accordion player is brought in to coax it out.

I didn't feel very good in there and went out into the garden, asked the Japanese curator about *the orchard*—could that also mean orchid garden? He replied that he didn't know whether orchids were ever grown in this house. I couldn't correct the misunderstanding. Bought some postcards and a recipe book, which included recipes for porridge and those lovely butter cookies, and also a flower book with the names of the flowers grown by the siblings, and more seeds to give to Owlie, so that maybe he can grow the British flower that resembles small gentian but is not small gentian, because it grows only in the north. Opens itself only toward a gentle sun.

The seats are littered with teenagers' old chewing gum, but it's a good feeling to be rolling along at high speed, facing forward. I'm on a train to Manchester. Was going to spend the night there and visit John Ruskin's home, Brantwood, which he renovated according to his ideas on organic architecture, designing the wallpaper personally based on his dreams and fantasies. Was then going to visit the home of Beatrix Potter, who wrote about Johnny Town-Mouse, who couldn't bear the quiet of the countryside, and Timmy Willie, the country mouse, who couldn't bear the bustle of the city. *One place suits one person, another place suits another person. For my part, I prefer to live in the country, like Timmy Willie.*

For now, I content myself with buying their books. Must come back here again soon. And then go farther north, and out to the islands. Have a look at the stone circles that are thought to be sundials, or calendars, associated with pagan worship of the solstices. Maybe there we have a stage for a new democracy, a draft version of a public forum. Solstice-democracy; how does that sound?

It would have been good to touch the stones now, because I feel as if I'm standing at a crossroads, a solstice. Maybe I would have been quicker to enter the new era if I'd made it to the stones, which are very close by. No regrets, I'm going as fast as I can and want to. Or, as William wrote:

> *No joyless forms shall regulate*
> *Our living calendar:*
> *We from to-day, my Friend, will date*
> *The opening of the year.*
>
> *Love, now a universal birth,*
> *From heart to heart is stealing,*
> *From earth to man, from man to earth:*
> *—It is the hour of feeling.*
>
> *One moment now may give us more*
> *Than years of toiling reason:*
> *Our minds shall drink at every pore*
> *The spirit of the season.*
>
> *Then come, my Sister! come, I pray,*
> *With speed put on your woodland dress;*
> *And bring no book: for this one day*
> *We'll give to idleness.*

And his sister writes in her journal that she and her brother lay together on the ground and listened to each other's breathing and to the water in the air, and that he said he imagined it would be like that in the grave, in complete quietude listening to the peaceful sounds of the earth, knowing that dear friends were near.

Under the yew tree. I wanted to lie there and take a long rest. Then get up and have gingerbread cookies in the gingerbread house, dip them in apple cider, as the squirrel on my shoulder hopped with joy and accidentally stuck a nut in my nose. Or what. I remembered the words of Eyowl, my sister in arms. When she was so inflamed, realizing the difference between our fight and an older one: No, not *back to nature*, but *forward*! Forward to nature!

I noticed the crows flying off, following each other, in a hurry. So I grabbed just one cone from my path and ran after them, bid farewell to the Lake District. Limped on one leg yet still made the bus, whose roof had been cut off, and I dashed about the sky and grazed the crowns of the trees with the crown of my head and the crows cawed in my hair and told me jokes about the future, how fun it would be to have my own home, arrange all my little things on the shelves.

Why didn't Dorothy just live with Coleridge, for example? Why didn't they create a platonic home together? Then they could have made a more dynamic connection with William's home. Instead, she focused entirely on him and ended up depressed from the intimacy that never really developed, after all.

Then I saw a little sign: Owl Area. I thought about depression and intimacy, what connection there might be between them. What about the owl? It lays its eggs in other birds' nests, often falcon nests, yet is dependent on no one. Was Dorothy too dependent on her brother? Was that the problem? Perhaps being dependent on intimacy, closeness, is just a short step from depression.

Then the phone rang. It was my ornithologist, calling to remind me that I'm a ptarmigan and must be careful of falcons! No, we didn't talk about birds then. He was on a pay phone and just managed to tell me that he'd come all the way to the British Isles, asked whether I might want to meet him. Was he kidding? I turned abruptly on my heel and ran to the train station in one mad dash, through white moss, panting. My mind spun, spitting and spouting, and I scolded myself, or tried to rectify my thoughts and hereditary day-night confusion, or whatever other confusion it was.

Oh, how inappropriate it is to dwell in mental masturbation, toy with the idea of living with your brother and his wife, in a wing of their house, a cubbyhole, writing and milking the goats. Now I have no time to lose! Go on, you frigid old bird, you over-boiled, foggy fool, the bells will fall silent and the stripes will fade on your cloven jester's cap unless you run now! Bing, bang, and boom, frog in a box and worm in a stream.

My legs wet, I meet my man; I must point out that it's not pee, just genuine British moor-damp. Turn to face him, straight on; no chickening out.

We'd arranged to meet in a library named after a certain Rylands, a pioneer in textile manufacturing and book collector. He said that it was Neo-Gothic. What's that? Neo-Gothic! I decided not to tell him on the phone, since I was out of change, but I am in fact reading about the Gothic spirit in Ruskin's book; it's a red, flowery book, decorated with leaves. In it, Ruskin boils the Gothic spirit down to several inseparable elements:

savageness
changefulness (variety, desire for change)
naturalism (close connection with nature)
grotesqueness (uninhibited imagination)
rigidity
redundancy

Insular ornaments. Island patterns? See, there I write "*mynstur*" (patterns) with a "y," so maybe the period during which I can't bear a "y" in "mynstur" and have to see it written with a "u," "*eyjamunstur*" (island patterns) is finished. It would be fun to be with a grammarian now and discuss this a bit; I would go and buy us crepes with cream and coffee and talk about islands and hospitality and patterned pillows beneath tired heads, and ornamented leaf-bread in hungry mouths. Come to mention it, I'm really hungry.

Sitting next to me is a middle-aged couple. The woman starts talking to me . . .

We had a good chat; they were getting off the train, gave me their address and invited me to come visit and stay whenever I wanted. I munch on barely-nutritious butter cookies. I'm planning to change my diet when I get back home, finding myself yearning for the good old healthy option.

I noticed that she had a necklace around her neck, and she said it had a Celtic pattern. She'd bought it in Orkney. ORKNEY? I exclaimed. She asked: Oh, what about it? I then told her about the kiln house in Iceland, which was Orcadian in shape, one of a kind, and that this Orcadian influence was still unresearched, for the most part. I didn't quite remember what the deal was, why it was so exciting to find out about Orcadian influences. I'd completely forgotten, but I said that I was going to write a book about it later. She replied reassuringly that many people would doubtless find such a book quite interesting.

Our conversation had actually come to an end. I added, just to clarify things, that before the Vikings sailed with Orcadian women to Iceland, there'd probably already been people living there: the so-called *papar*, Irish monks who'd sought peace and quiet on the island, but were later driven away with their bells by those arrogant rats, the Vikings. A momentary silence on the train. I hoped they wouldn't start asking me about the Icesave case.

She asked if I wanted to know how she acquired this neck-lace, which I'd actually been wondering, but wouldn't have dared to ask. Her husband said that it was a good story, which I'd probably find interesting, no less because I was so excited about the Orkney Islands. Yes, I certainly was.

She said that her ex-husband had drowned in a harbor in Orkney. He had been working as a diver at an oil refinery and had to repair a pump deep down in the sea, but his equipment failed and he drowned. She was at the site, waiting for him to surface. She waited and waited. Rubbed her gold necklace. On it is a Celtic ivy, which symbolizes eternal love because it crawls all the way up to the sky and carries messages between earth and heaven. Yes, with pentagonal leaves like envelopes.

Her second husband works on the same oil rig and said that the Orkney Islands are in fact a bleak place. There's nothing there. Maybe I should write a book about something else. I was going to mention the debate on natural conservation and the independence of island nations, their self-respect and how they let themselves be exploited in ass-kissing lameness. But of course I couldn't go into that on the heels of their terribly tragic story. Tears welled in our eyes when we said goodbye.

Well, then the train runs into the city, the industrial chimneys fart with old joy and the library will close in half an hour. I've got to run if I'm going to make it there.

The building is grotesque and clumsy-looking, but very beautiful. An ambitious, red toy castle with a million giant glazed windows, a nonagonal reading room and wise men who watch over the books. I said hello to Socrates, Shakespeare, and Newton. Searched for a woman but found none before the second floor, where there were two; one was theology herself, with her long hair, and the other the widow of the man who built the library, and who donated all of its books.

I was shy with Birdy, which meant that I naturally paid even more attention to all the small details therein; to the oak-leaf pattern on the printing press and the floor. He bought me a plastic ring in the lobby just before the doors were locked. Then we went to an apish bar and toasted our reunion. He looks so good in his new British shoes and white shirt, and said that he was happy to have changed his plan. He was halfway to another continent when he decided to make a U-turn and be with me this summer, instead.

When he said that he'd flown on the Iron Maiden plane, I pulled my book from my purse and read *Rime of the Ancient Mariner* by Coleridge; and yes, that's right, Iron Maiden had released a song by that name.

I had to admit to him that during my trip, I'd imagined him as Coleridge, who, as far as I knew, may have been the lover of both; well, or just a friend, a good friend, whether that really mattered to him . . .

Maybe he should have seen Dove Cottage, and their friendly little cave. Naturally, we could have rented a car and driven between the calendar stones, the stone circles found throughout the Lake Country. But we'll do that later. Now we're sailing up the canal, back to our village. Where we've been invited to stay for a while, on the outskirts of the city. Maybe it's the Hveragerði of England, our mix-ins not far ahead.

No mix-ins welcomed us, just endless greenery. And friends. Flowers had been put in a vase on a cardboard-box night-stand, and the bed made up for us. Tea and cookies before calling it a night, and anecdotes from our travels.

The house is big and quite unique in shape; numerous rooms, with secret routes between them. Every room has some peculiar furniture; a table that spits its center up when a button is pushed, a writing lectern with forty secret little drawers, and a dressing table that turns out to be a summer cottage for a toy family and animals. The house is located at the junction of the city and the countryside, and the garden surrounding it merges with the woods. And the stream that runs through the property is dammed for electricity; the garbage recycled.

In the kitchen there's an old gas or coal stove; I don't quite understand this phenomenon, but in any case, it can occasion-ally get very hot there, as in a steam bath. You sit and sweat and talk about the frogs in the garden, which are more tolerant than the ones you've known up until now, and about the women who hear their birthday songs sung at a higher frequency than they're used to.

It's a bit remarkable, experiencing this sort of coexistence. There are quite a few of us here, but we never crash into each other. Everyone does their own thing, their own work. One and all to his or her own rhythm. No one has ever talked about an overall organization. No one's set any rules, yet there's no discord.

At the start I wondered whether we all were spending so much time getting used to each other's presence that we maybe did nothing else. But that wasn't the case. Everyone just respects the others' need for privacy, effortlessly, but consciously. I think that most of us are investigating future forms of communication, each in his own way. Every one of us has created a working climate in his own space, and no one would dream of bursting through the others' invisible protective membranes. But then we meet from time to time, and somehow always end up in a fundamentally good discussion in the kitchen. And most often, it's a discussion about the future of cooperation, about trust and love.

I think that everyone living here now has had many years of training in respecting others' space; yes, I think that we could actually form a national team in coexistence. Eyowl is particularly good at listening for the rhythm of the day and tuning the strings. She aligns herself with the days' transformations and seems to perceive the flood and ebb tides, the undercurrents and confluences. Respects the nature of each moment in and of itself. My ears grow and I learn, become more sensitive to the nuances of the day.

We're all interested in working methods, in the construction of space, the world, the day.

Various guests come here as well, and they're always welcome, both invited and uninvited. Yesterday we all cooked together and had an excellent party. Birdy and I went with the kids to buy balloons and all kinds of other decorations.

At dinner I had a good conversation with the catlike Ludwig, about a new type of farming: *the vertical farm.* He describes it as a fluorescent green system based on transferring land to city dwellings. I'm not sure about that solution, which seems to be an interim one. Then someone named Meyvant told me how studies were being done on beehives, to learn more from them about architecture. I told him about the farmstead at Gröf in Öræfi, about the excavation that's one of the few sources for a long architectural period in Iceland and that my brother and I think might be an example of a constructional system that would be worth investigating. I also told him about the kiln house at Gröf, and it turned out that this Meyvant is an expert on such houses in the Orkney Islands. What's special about them is that the excess heat from the drying oven is channeled back and forth so that no heat is wasted; instead, energy is cycled throughout the entire cluster of farm buildings, meaning that, for little expenditure, heat can be maintained throughout the dwelling and power an entire mill, dry grain, and heat the sauna and cowshed. That's how the internal system of a romantic relationship should be! I cried triumphantly. That was it, precisely! To build up intimacy, as in a kiln house! He agreed and drew a rather complex picture on a piece of paper, which I put in an envelope to send express to Owlie.

Birdy was engaged in deep conversation, first with Tern, who explained to him the latest septic-tank and gas production research, then with the interesting Whimbrel, who has a beautiful long beak and can fine-tune hearts. Eyowl told me about her friends in Indonesia who moved from London to an island and built a house with waste material; it's like a cluster of little huts on a large plot, so their home is both outside and in and the houses are open and monkeys live with them. Yes, and speaking of waste material, said Eagle, I know a man whom I call Trashy, because he lives nowhere and travels around the world with his family on boats that he builds out of trash. He teaches his children himself, and provides for his family by utilizing the waste of consumer society. And then of course there are all the boat-people, who live on boats. It's a tempting option.

I missed Owlie and wrote him a long message and told him about all these speculations. About how we'd gotten a kind of home-academy going. How we live both externally and internally and find a balance in coexistence. He wrote me back and said that he misses his dear sister and asked when I was coming home. He's going with his family on a camping trip around the country. I hope that we can all meet and create a new farm with family and friends and all live together. In diligent and cheerful honey-scented warmth in the light of the latest insights.

I sleep well here and have gathered old poems of mine into a new book, rewriting them along the way, coming up with original material for them, allowing them to erode overseas and transform. Birdy has also been working well, mapping the birds in the village with great precision, and has added several sounds to his alphabet; now he can distinguish between a hundred and fifty. It takes time to learn bird language, as you might guess. I try to listen attentively to the songs but often confuse species.

We witnessed the birth of a new sound this morning. A new connection to the dimensions.

We've enjoyed having the kids come visit us sometimes in the mornings, the two foals, who whinny and laugh like children berrying and pull us out into the garden to gather leaves from the conjoined linden tree, its two trunks growing from one root. Then they run into the forest and hide, disappear and leave us on pins and needles, always so fearful that something will happen to them. We've got to let go if we're going to have our own child; it's useless to be so stressed. From somewhere in the forest we heard such a strange harmony that we re-tuned ourselves to each other for a moment. I felt as if together, we could do whatever we wanted to do. I felt trust crawl out of its egg.

I wonder whether this house might be built so well that I'd feel fine in it with anyone. Because you can always find peace and quiet out in the garden. But no, clearly both have to be all right: the housing and the company. And offer both privacy and intimacy. I'm not asking for much . . . .

Recently, the two of us have sometimes gone in the evenings to a little countryside pub and had porridge and sausages, liver and mashed potatoes. Have been chatting about life and existence. But tonight will be a real shakeup. The countryside gang is going to a big-city concert. It's none other than Mr. Dog who's taken it upon himself to shatter our quietude. I vaguely recall something and put on sunglasses, just to be sure.

O ur seats were in the best spot, with a great view over the stage. I was stunned by the atmosphere. It was a celebration of the twentieth anniversary of the release of a particular album, and I felt as if I were a hundred years old. At the same time, I felt the eternally young, fickle fool in me waken to life and laughter. Were these staging mistakes? On the stage was a bench exactly like those in the garden at Skógar and in the orchard of the Wordsworth siblings, but was supposed to be, I think, the studly bench in the hood in the big city.

The homeless dog remained sitting on the fine pine bench in a thick down jacket in fifty-degree weather and scratched his balls and kept on asking if everyone was having a good time, a blast. Ordered everyone to *put your motherfucking hands in the air*! Unfortunately, I still have that line in my head. Might have to have an operation to get it out, because the beat was so compelling.

In the taxi on the way home, I suggested to Birdy that we translate Snoop's lyrics into Icelandic, and asked whether we couldn't just translate *Doggystyle* as "a dog's mannerism." He asked in surprise whether I really didn't know what doggystyle meant. Oh, not the way a dog is? I asked. No, in general, it means the sex position *from behind*. Oh, I completely missed that. I mean the term, not the style. Is it an Irish word, originally? Joke. He suggested calling Snoop "Snati," which I think is a great idea. And here comes the first verse, which reminds me very much of my dear William's *Lyrical Ballads*, long and rhymed to death: *Homeless all around us and this we shan't belie: we mustn't let our brother homeless feel their spirit die. So give a shit with all you've got, it doesn't do to try—raise those motherfucking hands to the sky.*

WHICH JAMES? THE ONE THAT WAS IN MY CLASS
AT EASTSIDE ELEMENTARY? WHERE IS HE NOW? IT'S
PROBABLY ST. JAMES, A PILGRIM WITH A SHELL IN HIS
POCKET FOR DRINKING WATER ALONG THE WAY

So far I haven't managed to orient myself in London. But now we live on a boat out on the canal, where you see the city from a different perspective—from below. I'm able to get into it from here.

Next to our boat is one with a puppet theater; I went there to see a performance of Little Red Riding Hood and the Wolf, but felt sick from the rocking and left before intermission.

I walked past the hospital where my grandpa once had heart surgery. The doctors told him that he had to change his pace; he needed to relax, his heart couldn't bear the load. But he'd told Grandma that he was just going to keep going like before, until he dropped dead. And that's what he did. He'd been trying for many years to save the country, built numerous houses and factories, taught, published books, held countless lectures, tried to export Icelandic industry and had a lot of children. But there was always something left to do. He was a visionary, envisioned a new society, a sustainable society, but was just so far ahead of his contemporaries, the dear man, that no matter how fast he ran, he could never make it into the future.

Grandma came with him here to England, stayed in a guest-house quite some distance from the hospital and went to him in the mornings and sat with him all day, sometimes wrote in a diary, descriptions of people and reflections on the place.

Once when she came home from the hospital, she flipped through the phone book and found the surname of the man she'd loved as a young woman in the north, having newly completed her studies, before she got married. He was a literary man, but came to Iceland as a soldier, and somehow I can imagine that she'd never, either previously or afterward, met a man who was so able to appreciate her humor and her talents, her uniqueness. As far as I understand, they met in the room that she rented after she moved away from home to attend high school.

He had to leave with his unit. Go to a real war. The only news that she had of him was from his father, somewhat later; he wrote her and asked whether she'd had any news from him. No, nothing. She rang his number, but hung up.

I thought I saw him yesterday in an antique bookshop that sold beautifully bound books, about puppet theaters and British games, among other things. I was browsing a book with drawings by Beatrix Potter when a tall, slim, and polished man wearing a light wool overcoat and an unusual gentleman's hat tugged at my little tail, asked me to excuse the intrusion, but he simply had to say how amazing my hair color was; what sort of genes did I have, if he might ask?—like a blend of red and rat-gray.

I said that I'd inherited the red from my grandmother and namesake; she'd had fiery red, braided hair, and had been beautiful in her ice-skating outfit . . . I felt as if he would recognize the image; yes, don't you remember her little leather coat and how freely she glided over the ice? What if this were him, in the flesh, Grandma's gentleman, her first love?! During our conversation, I managed to slip in that I was from Iceland, but he said he'd never been there; hadn't gone any farther north than the Orkney Islands.

Yesterday, however, my first major and tragic love called, completely unexpected, and I went and met him; we had cinnamon rolls at the canal café, on the boat with the ivy. He's fathered many children, and has outdone his father. We didn't talk about our relationship at all, but a few images of us twenty years ago came to mind.

He was coming from a concert in Manchester, his mind totally blown, and he said that he'd even gotten goosebumps when an image of the tectonic plate boundaries at Þingvellir appeared; he who hates nationalism and patriotism. Þingvellir is a symbol of the friction between different forces in nature and in democracy. I recalled the debate that we had at Goðafoss waterfall the other year, when I tried to save the love of nature from the claws of nationalism. I remember that we argued all the way south in his grandmother's little Volkswagen. I was trying to make a clear distinction between nationalism on the one hand and patriotism on the other. But he said that it all turned out the same: in violence against foreigners and all who aren't categorized as sons of the fatherland. And now, twenty years later, we took up this same thread. I said that

that was absolutely right; the distinction between nationalism and patriotism wasn't clear enough. So I came up with new alternatives, taking only twenty years to find the right terms: *móðurjarðarást* or *móðurjarðarumhyggja*, that is, love or care for mother earth. I find them a bit beautiful—though maybe not very manageable. Maybe it'll take another twenty years to find better terms?

My coffee cup was very deep and the cinnamon roll a big spiral. Together, we rejoiced at having developed more trust in our love. We didn't put it that way; didn't mention love. Nor did we mention how we wrecked the trust between us back in the day. I couldn't eat, couldn't walk, and absolutely couldn't play the piano; I stopped learning to play it shortly afterward. We listened to Joy Division over and over, but it was all for nothing; we simply couldn't reconnect, didn't trust ourselves to do so.

But we didn't talk about it. Just about love in its broadest context, love of life.

I told Birdy about this conversation and about the new terms; the new distinction that was supposed to clarify our relationship with our mother earth in the future. We discussed it up and down and came to the conclusion that the distinguishing feature of mature love is an understanding of the entirety, of the overall impact of all actions.

I had crawled into my bunk, but had the tendency to clamber down again to put ideas on paper. Remembered the age-old concepts that still apply, and are better than *móðurjarðarást*: fosterland and love of the fosterland. Compare: *Serene and warm, now southern winds come streaming . . . .*

It's good to replace the idea of "love of one's native land" with "love of one's fosterland," to clarify your relationship to the country you tied your umbilical cord to. But won't you continue to be considered a nationalist if you say that the citizens of a country should be responsible for their fosterland and its natural resources? In such a case, there's more going on than just care for the fosterland. Or what? I actually think that care for the foster mother is inseparable from care for all its sons and daughters, whether they're related by blood or not.

Maybe soon we can invent a new corporate form. Until now, corporations haven't been based on collective responsibility. They have nothing to do with responsibility. In corporations, everyone thinks about their own shares, and no one is accountable to the whole. While we haven't yet come up with a proper way to make corporations accountable to nature and the public, while the shareholders operate beyond the bounds of justice, we can hardly trust individuals with large shares in our country. Nor, unfortunately, can we trust the government, as experience has shown. But perhaps we can come up with a new way to connect with nature and justice. Come up with a new collective form, a new form of shared responsibility.

Do I think most about sailing? Or about journeys in general? I was in fact reading these words of Uggi in *Ships in the Sky*: *It was because of my homelessness that I'd begun thinking. He who thinks is no longer bound to a certain area, to the land, or to a congregation. He is an outsider. He is all alone. He is free as a bird.*

I'm thinking about loyalty. Isn't loyalty to the fosterland different than loyalty to the fatherland? Loyalty to democracy and justice different than loyalty to a group or family? I'm not thinking about loyalty for loyalty's sake, like that claimed by sweaty, self-assertive SS hot dogs. That loyalty is ultimately very self-centered; it's about loyalty to one man's dream, disconnected from others. On the other hand, it seems to me that loyalty to the fosterland can't be separated from connections to the totality of all things.

Finally I made it to the Freud Museum, after taking a long time to get there. Birdy suddenly had a vague recollection of it as we sat together this morning and tried to plan our day.

On the landing inside the house was a little flower conservatory, easy chairs and a small desk with an encyclopedic dictionary open to a drawing of an orchid. I remember when I developed my passion for orchids and selected a black one that died too quickly in the dimness of my attic room in Paris. On the upper floor is Anna's bedroom, her father's daughter, and a photo of him above the bed! Under the watchful eye of her father, she conducted remarkable experiments in the field of psychoanalysis, but had the sense to be psychoanalyzed by people other than him, among others by a shared friend of hers and her father, Lou Andreas-Salomé; there's a picture of her on both floors. Down in the spacious office space of the papa wolf, in two adjacent rooms, you're first welcomed by Gradiva, "she who walks," and a black chalk drawing of two women with children, probably loving lesbians with only-begotten children.

On the shelf are snakeskin-bound stories by Marie Bonaparte; I could only read the words on one spine: *Printemps sur mon* . . . It was she who fought against the death penalty and saved dozens of Jews from the claws of the Nazis, bribed them so that Freud could make it out of Vienna alive. She was the first translator of his works into French and was introduced to his ideas there, a pioneer in psychoanalysis and had herself circumcised and her clitoris moved, as part of her years of attempts to achieve orgasm. A hexagonal table with candles and the recording of troubling dreams about a child that caught fire. The desk covered with little statues as a reminder of where the standards of our thoughts and dreams come from. There he is, my bronzed Osiris, and in another place his sister Isis, still searching for his penis; she won't give up, clever little thing. The son of these siblings is Silence, the hermaphroditic god of the spaces between words. And Bes, the copper-skinned dwarf, the cocky comic, protector of households, humor, sex, and dance. I really must get myself one of these ithyphallic Beses for our new home, if we actually ever have one someday.

Small, dancing clay statues like those found in graves in the Greek city-state of Tanagra, of chubby and beautiful women enwrapped in ivy and musical instruments. A wry midwife-crocodile and a bone-marrow drawing in lead. A small, copper Hathor and Athena with her owl; he called upon them during his flight from the Nazis. *They hold a protective hand over us*, he wrote to his wife, with whom he corresponded a great deal, I could feel the words on the soles of my feet because all the archives are in the basement, but I wasn't able to go there; you have to make an appointment ahead of time.

I wanted to lie down on the bed; the red velvet curtains reminded me of the living room at home when I was little. And the perforated seats of the wooden chairs. Imagine how well he arranged things; how he placed each book meticulously, every object, and then died just a year later. Which makes this like his mausoleum—and I even sense his consciousness of it; he scribbled on the wall of his grave, sick man.

The little shop in the Freud Museum was like a nightmare. There were several books about the master and his daughter, as well as beautifully made cards, but then the whole place was drowning in tasteless reproductions on drinking cups and slippers, as if you get something out of shoving your toes into the image of this remarkable man! I don't quite get this perverse impulse. Birdy was absolutely devastated, and said that as far as he was concerned, such a museum shouldn't need to be so desperate to sell things, it didn't need to stoop to the customers' banality. Still, I decided to buy a postcard, and waited in line a long time.

In front of me stood a curly-headed man, all sweaty in a wet, gray T-shirt, and the woman at the register was also curly-headed and he told her that he was an artist, worked in clay, as a matter of fact. Oh, what sort of pieces do you create? she asked, probably out of courtesy more than interest, though I really couldn't tell, but at least she probably hadn't expected such a detailed answer. He said that it would be complicated to explain, but some of his pieces hung on threads—clumps of clay; he tried to bring out patterns in them. I waited as he found the words for this artistry of his, impatiently at first, fiddling with my teeth, but then remembered being in such a fix myself, and my irritation was blended with sympathy. We're probably at the same anal stage, Curly and I.

When I first arrived in Paris and had to apply for housing at a particular office that I couldn't find, I practiced what I was going to say to the office woman several times before I finally made it to my destination. I was so nervous about explaining what I wanted that I'd prepared a speech, learned it by heart, and then just poured it out over a man who asked if he could help me. I wandered back and forth in the large lobby, while this man swept and listened to my rigmarole all the way to the end and smiled nicely and said that it was truly interesting and that the person I needed to talk to was there on the other side of the door. He waved and congratulated me on my interesting research, and then continued with his sweeping.

It's so embarrassing to think that someone is actually interested in what you're thinking. And in that regard, it's almost unbelievable that autobiographies are published. Who cares about your story? I bought a little book by Thoreau in a bookshop last night, with this statement on the first page: *I will therefore ask those of my readers who feel no particular interest in me to pardon me if I undertake to answer some of these questions in this book.* He wrote the book to answer questions that he was asked so repeatedly when he lived alone, far from all, and attempted to sustain himself by the labor of his own hands: aren't you lonely, afraid, how can you afford this?

I greatly enjoyed reading this book of his. And now I'm browsing through an essay that I found in the Freud shop. There I read that Cybele, the goddess of caverns, who was in fact enwrapped in ivy, loved Attis, after all; he who was born of an almond and fostered by a he-goat but cut off his own genitals. Because he listened to her so well. The sound of her voice healed the wound in his groin. And then it tells of Persephone, entwined by a green vine, with a pomegranate in one hand, and the other reaching for the hand of her mother Demeter. This mother-daughter pair continually renew their relationship. The daughter dies intermittently and makes her way down to Hades and dwells there in the underworld for a season. There she spends her time tending souls, wrapping bandages around the heads of the newly deceased, but then climbs vines back up, returns home and shares her experience with her mother, who always wants to hear her stories because her ears are the earth itself.

Today we visited bookshops. First went to say hello to a porcupine, sharpening its snout in doubts. We got lost in the biggest shop and when I finally emerged from the whirlpool and had given up on finding him, and was just about to step out onto the sidewalk, he came, looking upset, and asked why I hadn't gone to the shelf marked B; I should have known that he would go straight to the B, whereas it was impossible to know what section I would go to. I apologized and laughed at him, saying that I hadn't known he would only be looking for books by Thomas Bernhard.

We got over it quickly. Went to a café and showed each other our books. I bought two more by Ruskin. I don't understand how he could have gotten past me throughout my entire school career. A man whom I spoke to in Worsley said that a professor of his in Oxford had been obsessed with Ruskin and his ideas, dressed in exactly the same velvet clothing and spoke the same way that he wrote, adopted all of his mannerisms. I probably would have done the same if I hadn't read that Ruskin had likely been a pedophile.

Apparently, a large percentage of pedophiles were abused themselves, and their aesthetic and emotional growth stagnated at the age they lost their freedom. They try to regain their freedom by taking it from others of the same age they were when they lost theirs. Logical?

I woke Birdy tonight and asked whether he was a pedophile. Whether he'd been abused. He took my questions well, put his comforter up over my shoulders, asked me to try to go to sleep; no, he wasn't a pedophile, hadn't been abused. Didn't even ask why I asked. He's tolerant; said he thought I was diving a bit too deeply into whatever I was reading.

The city is unusually green right now. Pleasantly ugly and tediously spread out. No holistic city planning. Where is Guðjón Samúelsson's citadel? There's a very strong contradiction in me: on the one hand, preferring that all of the houses in the countryside be off-white with red roofs; a roof in an ugly color can actually make me feel physically ill. And if the church colors, creamy yellow, sky blue, and blood red are combined incorrectly, it can make me angry. On the other hand, I'm against all such aesthetic and systemic centralization. It's as if there are two building inspectors on duty within me, at the same time, each with his own plan.

I visited Grandma in her little room. She's excited about the pilgrimage that we're planning to undertake in the next few days. She asked whether Owlie was going to go with me. Yes, that had been the idea, but now he's tied down with work. I asked her to tell me once more about her housing situation when she was a child. And she described to me the attic where they plucked ptarmigan before going out and rolling in the snow, covered in feathers. But then she became confused. She was recently diagnosed with so-called day-night confusion, which means she loses track of time. Doesn't know whether it's day or night. Or what season it is. No matter how many clocks my daughters put on my nightstand, I don't know where I stand, she says with a laugh. I've got to shape up and get my life going in the right direction. Know where I stand, where I belong. I agreed with her: we namesakes were in the same place, or the same placelessness.

I brought her *The Bell Jar* by Sylvia Plath, in Icelandic translation. I warned her, saying that it probably wouldn't be the most upbeat reading, but she said that she was very excited to get to know the author. I left the nude woman on the book's cover on her nightstand, with all the clocks. We kissed each other goodbye.

In the corridor on the way out, I met an old mountain man who told me of when he first left home. He cycled over Hólssandur, got a good tailwind and was tremendously surprised to see the greenness and all the trees when he came down into Öxarfjörður fjord. He never saw any trees except for one gnarled little fir that didn't grow too well in the mountain air. Then he told me about Ravenna, about the mosaic there. And about a dream: When he went north to Fjöll and then over Haugur toward Vopnafjörður, but ended up in Ravenna! And now he tried to tell his family that if they couldn't travel abroad because of the economic crisis, it would suffice to go to Vopnafjörður. He's from there. I told him that my namesake was from there, too. Am hoping that they click and begin dating. It seems to me that there's not much action in this retirement home, or opportunities for courtship. It's like there's no space for flirting there.

It'll soon be the fall moving days. Feast of the Cross in the fall? Even sheep sorting. Dad can put any day into the context of world or local history: Now it's the seventh of August, when we got our first tractor, and the same day that El Salvador gained its independence.

In any case, we need to start looking for a place for the winter. The boxes of books are waiting, bursting with excitement. We've talked things over and agree that it would be best to create a proper home, now that we've decided to live together after all. We're on the lookout for our own land, and are going to take one little trip around the country to see what we can find. Even if it were just a small strip, we could possibly think of our future home in units, and start, for example, by building a kiln house somewhere on a heath.

I suggested that we go visit the places occupied by my forefathers and foremothers, on a kind of pilgrimage. Last year we went to check out his family's haunts. He was up for it and said that I should be the tour guide on our trip, but I immediately felt that I wouldn't be able to stick properly to schedule. But the main thing was to use the trip to gather elements from the soil to mix with our desire for a good coexistence. I decided to make a list of pros and cons in my family tree: What should be avoided and what taken as a model?

And here we find ourselves in Þingeyrar, where some of my lesser forefathers lived; I don't completely remember whom. Three pink mares met us as we drove up to the site of the long-gone monastery. I'd just been thinking about the convergences there at the sandbank where the monastery was built, imagining fish following currents from the British Isles and Europe and swimming straight into the sagas of kings and saints written down here in the thirteenth and fourteenth centuries.

I've wanted to stop here for a long time, have a look at the stone church with thousands of stars on its ceiling and thousands of panes of glass in its windows, but I don't remember why, particularly. Often when you've finally come to a place you've wanted to visit, you forget what made you want to go there. But it soon comes back to you. The church is more delicate than it appears from a distance, and lines itself up in smaller units that you can't find a place for in your heart until you're distant from it again. In retrospect. Vows are made at this church to St. Nicholas, to whom it's dedicated—the child-loving, obliging Santa.

I would really have liked to say a few prayers in this church, but it was so full of tourists that it had little air of sacredness. Yet the beautiful puppet theater beneath the gable did offer an opportunity for prayer. It escaped destruction during the Reformation, the official reason being lack of funds, but clearly, churchgoers didn't want to ruin this alabaster sculpture that housed their wishes, this beautiful stage for their hopes.

In the vestibule is a huge gravestone, engraved with a winged skull and three speartip-wounds, rusty since the time people searched for the judgment circle. Incredible that every effort hasn't been made to conduct archaeological research here, almost incomprehensible. The monastery was a hugely important hub of literary activity, producing translations and original writing. It's a pilgrimage destination for booklovers! Yet not one single book to browse can be found here. Tourism is strangely limited.

I asked the fellow who was showing the church whether he knew the people at the nearest farm, whence my great-great-grandmother came, along with the name Oddný. Once I was told a story of shame; a blight on farm and family. And when I clambered over the farm's horse fence to visit the family grove, called Oddný Grove, which had red-currant bushes and rowan trees, I got such a terrible electric shock in my thigh that I started thinking immediately about this shame. No, he hadn't heard this story, this fellow.

I found it remarkable to have a sense of family pride, or whatever it's called, for the first time, to feel my family honor wounded by some trivial story about the locals' carelessness, even irresponsibility and arrogance toward visitors. Did someone die at the doorstep? No, he hadn't heard of anyone doing that. I've got to ask someone else. Yes, strange to let such a thing be of any concern, but that's what age does to you. I was immensely relieved when the boy said he'd heard that my great-great-grandmother had been a loving, fair, and good woman.

The red in my hair probably comes from this place. It reminds me of the red of the berries, the current, and the beach where the messages in bottles wash up. It's just as well to recall the electrical shock, as a reminder of humility and eternal hospitality, if I ever discover in myself a trace of chieftainly arrogance, because most of my ancestors here were apparently important people in the district. I felt regretful as I walked across the hayfield, and cursed the way in which the country's rural areas have regressed. Where is the spirit, the self-sufficiency, the hospitality, the plucky and independent-yet-humble bearing?

I honestly have no desire to go back to the golden days. If someone was a chieftain, it was most certainly at the expense of others; injustice and inequality were and are so ingrained. But I would prefer it if the best from the ancient past, a certain attitude toward the countryside and industriousness, had developed differently, so that we could take up the frayed thread without needing to dig deep for it.

Instead of wanting to make everyone major farmers, enlarging their sheep sheds and increasing their debts, forcing them all to take on part-time jobs as truck drivers, we could instead give more people opportunity to have their own land, no matter how small, and to be self-sustaining and satisfied. Instead of digging up or tearing everything apart with excavators and building yet another tourist center. A barn, for instance, could be converted into a research center that based its activities on the ancient arts. Pray and work. *Ora et labora*. It's possible to work on something besides an excavator.

Earlier, we tried to find the judgment ring, without success. My dear Birdy is out in the car, chatting with his father on the phone. I'd better get going, am spending too much time copying down information; yes, the greatest book production in Iceland was carried out here, as well as care of the sick and the poor. A sanatorium and literary center in the same place!

I've got to remember to find *The Prophecy of Merlin*, from *Bretasögur*, and read it when I come to town. And a plaque here reads that Bergur Sokkason was the most renowned writer in the fourteenth century—composing, among other things, the sagas of St. Nicholas and the archangel Michael. I must admit that I'd never heard of this Sokkason.

I called Owlie to ask him about the shame story, whether he'd heard of anything disgraceful done at the doorstep here, but no, he couldn't recall any such story. I remembered a grandfather of old, Mála-Ólafur, who supposedly argued against the death sentence for Agnes and Friðrik, unsuccessfully. We always thought they'd been sentenced for incest. Where did that misunderstanding come from? In any case, their love was passionate. And, yes, criminal. I spoke to my namesake, Owlie's little daughter, on the phone; she's a truly wonderful being. They're together in the countryside now, the little family, and he said that he'd already harvested turnips and rutabagas. Well, the car is waiting, the journey continues. Next stop: Blönduós. I nearly moved there the other day—noticed a place for rent for cheap, with such a charming description: *Centrally located and much to see*. No shortage of irony there! I'd forgotten that my great-grandfather and grandmother lived there for a while. Built themselves a house there, but then moved to Reykjavík. The given reason: poverty. That's all I know. But the story of how he built the house is kind of nice in its retelling by Þórbergur, who heard it from the dean, and Dad reminded me: Gvendur the Triller was helping Great-grandpa, tossed his hammer up in the air and said that the house was to be centered on the place where the hammer landed.

We stopped at the retirement home and visited my great aunt. I bought roses, seven of them, reddish-orange fire. Birdy came up with the idea of bringing the same number as the siblings, and I had to call Dad to ask how many there were. Then, on our way up the stairs, I went over our family tree in my head. She welcomed us but said that she didn't have anything to offer us, and I regretted not having bought chocolates for her to offer to visitors.

On the wall was an ivory rose, an embroidered picture of composers, Schubert and company, and a mosaic of a winter ptarmigan. She said that she rocked and hummed to herself in her solitude, and, in a clear, high voice, sang us a verse about the fiddle that still sounds. She said that she'd often been asked to entertain people with her singing and poetry at evening gatherings in the countryside, and she'd always done so. She'd always loved singing so much, just like her mother and father, yes; they'd been great ones for singing and poetry. I recalled then that my great-grandmother was her mother, and I pulled something from my purse and gave it to her: an old embroidered cloth, cross-stitched with the inscription: *Towel 1919*. She looked it over carefully and respectfully. I told her that a certain good Ketilsdóttir had given me this treasure; Great-grandma had been working for her father and left the embroidery behind at his place. It would be most appropriate, of course, for you to have it, I said, since she was your mother. She abruptly folded up the poor little cloth and said, very firmly, no thanks, I can't take it, dearest. Because she left me behind, she left me, the darling. They never came to see me afterward, just left, she said somewhat brusquely, though with an apology, saying that she could be a rather harsh-mouthed person. Her belief is that if people have children at all, they should raise them themselves, no matter how poor they might be.

My siblings came to visit me; yes, it was fun when your grandfather entertained us, we recited poetry together and he played his instrument and I sang; he taught me our father's favorite songs; I guess he really admired Steingrímur Thorsteinsson and Þorsteinn Erlingsson. I asked if she had children; I couldn't remember. No, he could never get the old woman pregnant, folk said. But he was very handy and sweet, my husband, and a master carver, like Dad. I said that I knew shamefully little about these people, because my dad, like her, had been raised in a foster home. Your dad pretended not to have much interest in his "real family," as they say, though he's come here often and asked about his father. And I tell him all I can. Grandpa sent us a fancy Christmas card that he made in his workroom, where there were loads of ink bottles and rolls of paper. I wanted to live there, I said.

She asked how we were getting along; oh, of course, unsettled, I might have guessed. Sang a song about the gusty winds of life and felt so dizzy that she had to lie down. Asked me to hold her hand. I said that I was going to leave that afternoon and go out to the grazing sheds where our shared grandfather died. Ah, yes, the blessed man. He died there alone, but his daughter was with him in his old age, and was good to him. I'll never forget when my husband was asked if his wife was from that family, that rabble. And then those same people called on me to perform for them! I never said no; they just cursed us out of habit. My brothers said that I had my mother's voice. And now I just sit here humming and rocking; it's terribly nice, just humming and rocking like this. Yes, go on up to the ruins, my dears, and try to touch his soul through the earth; I think that would be a good idea. How very unlucky it was to die in someone else's grazing shed, and not in your own home. He was driven from home, and afterward never had land of his own. People may not realize now how important it was to have your own land in those days. Without it, you were nothing.

I asked whether she knew about the curse that the elf woman was supposed to have laid on our ancestor, which led to his family being splintered to the fifth generation; rootless, landless, restless. Yes, she certainly did know that story. Heard it from strangers when she was abandoned, far from the mirth of her poor family. Can't you forgive your mother? I asked, perhaps carelessly, but she took it well. Yes, I think I'm prepared to forgive her. Though I'm not sure. They were of course just renters, and had no space of their own to raise their children. I bought land with my husband, out here by the sandbanks, which was a huge blessing, but then I never had children. That's how inside-out everything is.

She thanked us sincerely for visiting her, though she regretted having nothing to offer us, a bite to eat or some sweets. But look at this ptarmigan. Yes, it's beautiful, I said. Our niece made this picture. She traveled with her father, Dad's brother, throughout the country. They did a lot of performing at popular poetry gatherings. We could have made such a trip, but Dad hadn't been so practical-minded, the blessed dear. He was clever in other ways. Is the house they built here in Blönduós still standing? No, it was demolished a long time ago. Everything's been demolished . . .

We were both quite silent on our way over the heath. I was wondering whether we should turn back and go to Bjarnarfjörður in Strandir, to my great-grandmother's farm, to Klúka, or to Svanshóll. Ohhh, where the sorcerer lived who was so opposed to the Church that when he died, he managed to squeeze out of his coffin and into a pagan grave mound in his farmyard? asked Birdy excitedly. I didn't know. We'd already passed it, anyway. Maybe we should go there on our next trip? he asked, and yes, I saw that that would be more doable, given the time we had.

He then asked me to tell him about this great-grandmother of mine. I remembered shamefully little. Except that she'd been working on a farm in the north and saved someone's life, was awarded a medal for rescuing a drowning man and dragging him back to his house, without being able to swim herself. Then she was a housewife at Grímsstaðaholt in Reykjavík, and enjoyed inviting friends and people from her district to her home to recite ballads with her, her husband, and their children. Someone told me that she'd actually kept the ballad tradition going at a time when people were mostly inclined to forget it, embarrassed by the awkward, outdated tone, the meter. The gatherings at her home, a kind of Sunday salon, laid the foundation for the Poets' Society. Great-grandpa had a cylinder phonograph and recorded the ballads, besides publishing books. They knew countless different melodies and could braid ballads together without end, for entire days, entire nights. Oh, why didn't my great-aunt get to be with them?

After crossing the heath, we wandered out through the tussocks and looked around for the ruins, following the instructions of the cultural heritage manager. But the fog was so thick that it was hard to see anything except up close. On one hill were field gentians and moonwort, a few alpine fleabanes, and snow gentians, making me think it likely that this was where he lay. I wanted to recite one of his poems, but couldn't remember any at that moment. Pretty darned typical. But Birdy came to my rescue and recited a dusky-metered one as we looked around for more ruins:

> *At dusk of my life's eventide,*
> *I peer ahead, there to behold*
> *beyond my grave, gaping, cold,*
> *runes so clear I'd carved this side*
> *upon my shield of hope untold.*

We walked back through the tussocks in the fog, listened to the bleating. Then his poems came flooding back to mind.

We drove up to the memorial at Bóla, where he lived. The road once passed by here, but now it's lower.

The stone harp is covered with a type of lichen that I think is called *glæta*, a copper-colored growth; I looked it up in the big book of fungi. There's a great deal of vernal grass and wood cranesbill here, beneath the sisters of the yew trees. Deep groves and tranquility. We pitched our tent outside the fence. It's raining hard and I think we'll have to set off early in the morning. I can't write any more at the moment because we forgot to buy a lantern. Wet matches and not a single shot of Brennivín. *Light in the darkness have I none.*

My namesake, my grandmother, told me before I said goodbye to her the other day that our hallmark was to remain unruffled. Never complaining. And maybe I should mention that the poet who rests here was rather peevish. I recall how, at our family reunion, people seemed pretty quick to pity themselves. Others were blamed for one's own failures, even elf women, if there was no one better to blame. I've got to be wary of this tendency. Write it down.

It should be borne in mind that justice in this country in the nineteenth century was little better than injustice, and maybe it's just as well to leave behind a reminder of injustice in one's poems, for other generations to remember how it was. This poet was driven from his dwelling, where he lived with his beloved wife and children. The farmers around him coveted his hayfields and accused him of stealing sheep; it was easy to come up with such lies since he was grouchy and looked like a wildman. But nothing was ever proven against him, no evidence was discovered and there were no witnesses, no trial. His reputation was in shambles and his family was without a home.

Upon my shield of hope, I carve a prayer for more justice. For people, animals, and the earth. And that the best from mother earth and the fatherland will guide me in my householding. Carve runes to remind me to be bold of heart. But how very beautiful melancholy can be when it's so near the earth.

I picked vernal grass off the grave and took it with me, feeling as if the fragrance brought me closer to the old days. But there's apparently a hole in the distaff side of the family, an inherited geographical confusion, and although I stared hard at the map, we drove past the birthplace of the woman whom I learned the other day was the grandmother of my great-great-grandfather . . . . His grandfather was supposed to have been a French sailor, from Étretat. When my great-great grandfather once visited the grave of the woman who was said to have been his grandmother, he supposedly recited a verse that I remembered was beautiful, yet couldn't recall, except for one line that I repeated to myself because it rolled around in my head—my poor driver, to have to endure this obsession: *in mold our honor lies, in mold our honor lies . . .*

Here in the hut where we're staying tonight, the poetry collections are in their places, and to my relief, I find the verse:

> *There by our ancestresses' graves*
> *in mold our honor lies.*
> *May our name live on and rise*
> *above the flashing, towering waves.*

On the way up here to Fjöll we saw the shepherd's hut where Mountain-Bensi sought shelter for himself and his livestock during storms. I remember when I brought my friend the old birdwatcher and farmer there, along with the accordion. Because I had a crush on the cook at the summer hotel, or just had a crush on the summer. We sat there for a while in the lava that bright night, singing songs. Smell of light.

For quite some time, I've felt ashamed of myself for having asked him to play *Blessed are you, dear countryside*. At first he refused, saying that it was sung over the graves of people from the Lake Mývatn area. But I wouldn't give up, thought he should play it anyway, in memory of Mountain-Bensi. My foster grandfather was christened after him, I think. Otherwise, all the details are quite hazy at the moment; along the way I was trying to educate my wise Birdy, who asked about this and that but generally got nothing from me.

We were relieved to be able to stay in the dry turf hut up here on the heath; the tent was too wet to put up happily. We're no longer Eggert and Bjarni, and anyway, they never came so far together; Bjarni covered the Northeast by himself.

The bridge over Jökulsá River, which Dad's real dad and foster dad had a hand in building, is white and powerful. The glacial river is strong and dirty and I always remember the ferryman with chills and admiration for his daring. Sveinn Pálsson describes one such risky crossing in a small boat and admits to having been terrified when he looked into the current, but just had to let go and trust. Then came the bridge, and Grandma took a taxi from Reykjavík all the way north; sped over the bridge with Dad in her arms. She'd gone and fetched him from her little sister in Reykjavík.

I could hardly believe my own words when I told Birdy that we actually had no family roots up here in Fjöll. Our nerves don't always extend outward from their family roots. And although Dad didn't want to be a farmer and left home early, he always wanted to come here to the north whenever he had time off; and he still wants to, in fact. North north north, we would always go north.

The other day Owlie said that he'd only recently appreciated just how unique the desert areas of the North are; in the South, almost every little strip of land is inhabited. He always wants to go north, too, whatever the weather. The other day when it was reported that some filthy rich Chinese businessman was going to buy up all the land here, he called me and said that he never would have believed it possible to recite the verse of the Mountain Poet with such sympathetic insight: *Now the North is gone from my sight, now I have no home.* I sincerely hope that people stand together and refuse to sell. Because what do we know about the buyer's intentions? Is it right, in general, for such a vast tract of land to be owned privately?

Private ownership of vast tracts of land appears to be an anachronism. We've got to rethink the relationship between private ownership of the land and public ownership of resources. Finally, water is being legally classified as a resource. But what about the desolation, the beauty and the spiritual space, the atmosphere?

I remember when my Owlie said in the spring, after we'd been collecting goose eggs, that he was realizing that ownership of land is of vital importance in life, and the fact that Dad had no claim to any land really haunted him. I laughed and said that I thought land ownership was a thing of the past; obsolete thinking. It would be quite enough for us to be able to come here to this turf hut when we wanted, where we could nurture our memories in peace. While he and our dad were building their turf hut, my mom and I were sauntering around Rome and Paris. We stayed in artists' residences and felt it easier to travel from place to place than to attach yourself to one particular heath.

Now I see that I was wrong. The Chinese businessman's offer has opened my eyes to a vision of the future. The connections to the land will not be severed so lightly. Nor will they be maintained unless they're cultivated, just like the earth. Do you have to own the land if you want your connection to a place to endure? What does Confucius say about that?

You might be able to enjoy the very best of it without actually owning it, as long as whoever owns it isn't going to use the land in a way that does harm to others. If you want to have something to say about land utilization, you've obviously got to own land. Such is the situation.

Earlier, we went down to the farm to fetch water, because the pond is dry. Were offered coffee and had a look at an old land map and talked about the Chinese businessman's offer. An intermediary had told the residents that the offer was exceptional and that it was now do or die; to hesitate was to lose.

The explanation given for this Chinese businessman's interest in Iceland was an Icelandic sweater knitted for him thirty years ago.

I completely understand how people are enamored with those who say they're going to produce and develop. It's only natural. Not least if the development benefits the locals. In a place where televisions explode due to unstable diesel generators, and where there's only enough hot water for short showers. I tried to convince them that they could become sustainable in other ways, not under the wing of the corporations. Because the ideal of sustainability is not about subsistence farming for everyone. Rather, that the farming is done in the interest of the earth, allowing the earth to provide coming generations with as much as it provides now. These speculations of mine were well received, though their flaws were quickly pointed out and I was offered a sausage.

But I remember when Dad, exhausted after having called for an open debate at Hrossaborg, said that in this place, as in so many others, people were always pressured to keep quiet. He respected the old farmers, but said that he'd thought about this for a good long time and yes, this term definitely applied to the place where he'd grown up: suppressive patriarchy. With hand gestures, he described how anything uncomfortable was smoothed over, just like the tussocks in the fields; just flatten them and cover them with turf.

Then is your turf hut a reminder of that suppression? Well, I don't know. Maybe a warning. Yet more a symbol of being able to live undisturbed by the patriarchy. To be able to live up on a heath and say whatever you like! And look at whatever you like; do nothing but stare at the mountains. It should be small enough, your hut, that it's impossible to do anything else but think and look at the mountains. The Chinese businessman is apparently a great fan of solitude and desolation. And what if he sells the land to someone who isn't as great a conservationist as he himself claims to be?

Might this potential sale be the logical outcome of the decades-long, incessant work of farmers that takes consumerism as its basis? We were reminded then of Jón of Möðrudalur, who wasn't considered a particularly good farmer—always a bit odd. He sent Dad a long, poetic letter about musicology and regularly called Grandma on the rural phone to ask how she liked some new song that was on the radio. And whether she agreed with him that Herðubreið looked most beautiful from Möðrudalur. No, she didn't agree. As a child, I thought it looked most beautiful from here, but as a teenager I revolted against that view and found it most beautiful from Möðrudalur, as asymmetrical as a newly-budded breast.

I t's rather cold outside today, and we've hunkered down inside the cabin to read. Birdy chopped wood for the fire; it's burning hot in here, and cozy. He's reading another book by Thomas Bernhard, *Correction*, about Wittgenstein's doppelganger, who plans to build his sister the perfect house. Wittgenstein came to Iceland back in the day, and traveled the country on horseback with a friend. Among other things, he was apparently looking for his own piece of land. Then he built a hut on a mountainside in Norway, a tiny hut where he could be alone with his thoughts. I find it quite incredible how much peace and quiet a person actually needs in order to devote himself entirely to his thoughts.

Now I'm reading a report by Owlie, who was born the same day as Wittgenstein. His report on research into the origins of the settlement at Hólsfjöll. When I lived in Paris and learned that he was going to dig himself down into the ground in the north, like a dog after an invisible bone, I admired him for the joke; for that absurd act and for wanting to follow the philosophers into the unknown, searching for relics in a cold, windswept land. Various people tried to dissuade him. But he was more stubborn than the devil, and got down to work with his tools and dug a hole all the way into the tenth century. The place has probably been continuously inhabited since then.

He headed the investigation at Hóll, even farther out here in the wilderness. They've been good together, he and his goat-farmer friend, roaming around the farm and recounting its stories. Owlie told me in the spring that we siblings should really set up our farm there. A goat farm. It would be our place; he was thinking of making an offer and building us a house where our families could live, and Dad and Mom and our grandmas could come and live with us, too. I liked that idea very much. We could even drag an old printing press out there to the ends of the earth. But these dreams were being discussed before the Chinese businessman drove up the price . . .

In the report, he tells of a folktale about the first settlers at Hóll. There'd been a certain Guðrún from Jökulsárhlið, the quick-witted Mountain-Gunnsa, who was outlawed when it was discovered that she was carrying her brother's child, went to the mountains with two goats, dug herself into a hill and then farmed the land, fished for trout, and built up a flourishing abode. Then her brother came to her, along with their other siblings, and they lived in peace and harmony for many years, far from human habitations and in defiance of the law.

Sometimes it's hard for people to understand why others seek out such remote places, except in utter distress. Meaning that no account is taken of beauty, and peace and quiet are valued at nothing. As are other means of farming.

Owlie's report explains his theory of the so-called grazing-shed economy. The grazing sheds made it possible for people to graze their livestock in the winter. Instead of keeping their animals inside, they hired manly shepherds to stay with their sheep up on the heaths, even for several years at at time. I find it a bit amusing how he describes masculinity so enthusiastically in the report: the independent shepherd.

I remember when the consultant walked with Grandpa out onto the hayfield, and when he returned he concluded that the hayfields were frostbitten. Grandpa trudged back, and looked gloomy as he offered the consultant mutton with milk. This judgment felt to me like a death sentence, and Grandpa seemed ashamed. As if he were responsible for the cold and the frost. As if he himself had become infertile.

Grandpa couldn't imagine land as useful for anything but farming. And he bequeathed his own land solely to his sons who intended to become farmers, while his daughters and his sons who'd left home received nothing. According to custom.

I've got to ramble on a bit here in my diary so as not to bore my cohabitant, despite his being a wonderful fellow-rambler. I simply can't always be bothering him when he's reading, even if I'm reading or thinking something fantastically important. But my buzzing is about the decline of this place. The big sheep sheds are like a memorial to a miserable farming movement. The large-scale farming movement, big-industry movement. Why not cottage industries, small-scale farming, in a different economic system? There are no subsidies for slow development; everything has to happen immediately, has to be big. Instead of nurturing small, independent units in mutually beneficial arrangements, farmers latched onto an expansionist agenda that faced no resistance but its own decline, which was predictable, because its aim was never to make farming sustainable.

I think farmers should be psychoanalyzed, and rethink their connections with the earth and masculinity. And not just farmers. All of earth's foster children need to learn to foster her.

We're going to drive over Sandur tomorrow morning. Then head north to Vopnafjörður, the opposite direction from our dear Kristján the Mountain-Poet. Hopefully the verse will be turned around and the North won't vanish from our sight.

We drove into Ásbyrgi and were alone at the pond with the widgeons. I remember when I sat on a rock out in the pond when I was nine years old, and thought that this would be a good place for thinking. There's a great echo at the bottom of the basalt bowl and I wanted to let Birdy hear it, but couldn't bring myself to disturb the serenity. The wood-cranesbill flowers have fallen and the berries are ripening. We picked and ate them as we walked along the horseshoe canyon. Birdy felt it remarkable to have an emotional stake in this beautiful place. We didn't feel like tourists, because to me, it was as if I owned a bit of it and could share it with him. But then I remembered an ominous episode. When the reindeer were driven off the bar. We stopped eating the berries, thought they tasted of blood.

When I stood at the doorstep of the old house where Great-grandma lived with her children, an official suddenly turned up, and happened to be an old schoolmate of mine in philosophy—he'd become a National Park ranger! Are you interested in this house? It's where the rangers live; a good house, a fertile house. He was chieftainly and offered us lodging and food, and said he had a good wife and two sons. They told us about life in the countryside. How it gave them ever more insight into society and helped them to appreciate it better. They really looked forward to attending the midwinter feast. They're doing an excellent job in everything, it seemed to us, and we admired them for having abandoned the city and embracing country life, with style; making hay and jam and whatever it might be.

They lent us a good pair of birdwatching binoculars and pointed out a place for us to monitor the grebes, with their red tufts, at the Ástjörn summer camp. I wanted to find the path the sisters took with the goats, where they always saw the short-horned owl in the shrubbery. But I didn't find it, couldn't get my bearings. But I found flowers that I've never seen before and that don't grow extensively in this country, heath-yellow meadow vetching, beautiful immigrants that hook themselves to the edges of the hayfields.

Grandma once said that she regretted selling her share in the farm, the strip of land she inherited from her mother. Great-grandma was a pioneer in woman's rights, sent her daughters for education and bequeathed her land to them. After she became a widow, she and her children slaved away and bought the land from the government and never needed any help from the district—she owned the land debt-free.

Dad remembers her well; they were great pals and she asked him to promise to ensure that the land never be sold away from the family. But by the time the Icelandic Environmental Protection Agency made a purchase offer, none of them had any plans to go and farm there. Grandma must have been satisfied that the land would be part of a national park, said Dad, with a doubtful look. Grandma sold not only her share in the land, but also the clay-bright mare and the foal. It's perhaps due to that regret that she has no intention to sell the share she has now.

It was inspiring driving up to the farmhouse. I was nervous along the way, asked Birdy repeatedly if we should turn back; it's bad to be disturbing people, come barging onto private property, snoop around out of curiosity. But he encouraged me to sit up straight, then jump out and introduce myself. Which I did; there was no going back. And the woman who lives there now gave me an extremely warm welcome. She's recently quit farming and is planning improvements to the farmhouse and land. The old house in which Great-grandma and Grandpa lived collapsed in the big earthquake. But they built a new one, and now own the land debt-free.

We walked with her around the old sheepfold. She told me about her interactions with my great aunt, with whom she sometimes exchanged stories and berries. The berries were sent south with greetings from mother earth, and the stories were sent north with greetings from a woman with a good memory. Stories about the farm from the time when there were windmills, a home generator, trout in the pond, and plenty of visitors. When plants were used for making dyes and medicines, and ptarmigan saved people's lives. She remembered everything about her childhood haunts so much better when she ate berries from them. There's something magical about berries. And one story from out in the world slipped in, from when my great aunt was in school in Norway, and she went to the home of Quisling to repair a wall hanging. The householder was excited when he discovered she was Icelandic. Was she familiar with leader-sheep? Good heavens, her father worked very hard on improving his stock, including trying to cultivate the leader-trait in sheep. She said that she'd been terribly surprised to find out that this breeding enthusiast was a Nazi. Then she described the wall hanging and how she repaired it.

We were going to ask if we could have a look in the old churchyard, but it had been plowed over. Oh? Yes, to make it easier to spruce things up around it. Now it's a hayfield. Damn my eyes. In mold our honor lies. I thought that she was buried there and felt quite sad, though it didn't take much for that to happen. My great-grandma, the midwife who went around the district and delivered children, also took matters into her own hands when some sheep got stuck in slush and were in dire straits, and it was too far to the next slaughterhouse. She had the sheep slaughtered in the district church and the meat distributed to everyone. Your grandmother is probably buried in the other churchyard. Oh, all right. I was relieved. But I still felt sad.

The farm is truly beautiful, although history is slipping from its moorings to it. Lava and tussocky heaths, mountains in the distance, and then the sea.

We walked out to the beach. Had a look at what had washed up. Are now at the café in the local museum, where Great-grandma's hand-sewn wedding dress is on display. And there were also clever embroidered slippers and eyeglass cases decorated with images of leaves, books bound by the district bookbinder, who bound every single booklet from the district and every little book that the Reading Society bought, mostly foreign books that folk in the area translated themselves and published in small quantities. He also made nice fur hats. Whose head holds such knowledge now? Under what fur hat? But now, just as there's a resurgence of interest everywhere in using local raw materials in design and production, the machines no longer work and the knowledge is in the grave.

W e drove out to the village of Kópasker and bought some local produce—cured lamb meat—before taking the new road all the way to Vopnafjörður. A new guardrail on both sides for the entire length of the road. That must have been a great relief job, said Birdy, and I reminisced on the time when Owlie and I were fence-building and our cousin was such a big man that he thought he could boss us around. We retaliated by talking to each other in the nonsense language we learned from Pinocchio, the little artificial man. Chatted about this, that, and the other, flora and fauna and clouds, but my cousin thought we were planning a revolt and started feeling insecure, and insisted that we teach him the language.

We're in the Eyri Restaurant in Þórshöfn, having gone for a swim and a soak in the hot tub, where you can read plastic-covered information about the village and how the locals once hung some French sailors.

Although this isn't a place or time for writing, I simply must get one thing down on paper: what I was thinking on the way over Melrakkaslétta.

When we protested how Icelanders sold their third-largest energy company to a foreign corporation, which had taken advantage of a gray area in the legislation, besides having a bad business reputation, a lot of people asked me if I'd really become such a big nationalist. And two men said they supported me since they were dedicated to Nazism, truth be told. This crosses my mind now because I know I'll be asked what I have against the Chinese businessman.

I have nothing against him or Chinese people in general. I've seen more Chinese movies than American ones, I think. But China is a superpower, and within its framework, corporate capitalism thrives. It's a colonial nation that doesn't hesitate to crush small states like Tibet, drive tanks over libraries and monasteries, hospitals and schools. Similar to the Vikings when they crushed the Irish monasteries on their way to Iceland. Karmic revenge?

If you're opposed to selling your country's chief resources, its energy and unique wilderness, to big businessmen and corporations planning large-scale projects, you're hardly guilty of nationalism. Nationalism, or Nazism, is distinguished by how, in the long run, it perpetrates violence against individuals, against the homeland, against small-scale farms. Everything for the one big farm. For expansion. Expansion for the sake of expansion.

Even if you support Kópasker's processing of lamb meat, it's a rather far cry from considering Icelanders to be better than anyone else, from a genetic or cultural point of view. A very far cry, if you think about it . . . but I find it good to be prepared with an answer, because when you find yourself in the trenches of county politics, there's no checking the earmarks very carefully; it's just shoot between the ears, straight into the animal's third eye.

VOPNAFJÖRÐUR,
JUNGLE DAYS AND SAILBOATMAS

We pitched tents beneath the cliff where Grandma used to make mudcakes as a girl. A good camping ground, with access to electricity and hot water, a shower and toilets. And a view over the fjord. The mackerel smell doesn't bother us and the factory's purr is pleasant; we just hope the profit goes into the pockets of the locals or those who do all the work.

On our way here yesterday we took a detour out to Langanes. The Sauðanes Museum was closed due to circumstances beyond control—probably the sun. I felt a pang of anticipation in my heart as we drove along the wild and unfamiliar coast. I felt bad disturbing the haymaking, etc., but still wanted to see him again after all these years. As the young farmer he was. The young farmer whom Owlie and I called Tarzan because he resembled the actor who played him; we were crazy about the movie and pretended to be Tarzan and Jane and developed an ape-language . . . when I told Birdy, he asked awkwardly whether we hadn't taken it too far. Too far how? I didn't understand what he meant. I understand it now; yes, it's a bit embarrassing. No, no, we didn't take it too far. We just said *oo oo* and *oo oo oo*, the same system as the rural phone, one short and two long for this farm, three short for that one.

But we were surprised when the new farmer in the district came to the door of the sheep shed, holding a rust-brown lamb with a broken leg that he'd found among the tussocks. He looked like Tarzan in his leather dungarees and wool sweater. We found him captivating.

I felt my ape urges awaken as we drove up the driveway and I saw him on his tractor, busy with his organic farming. I wonder if he's still in his leather dungarees? Naturally, one must protect one's sensitive scrotum in such stony conditions.

I thought he might come and greet his visitors, but he probably figured we were tourists and that his daughter would see to us. Instead, his wife, the tremendously beautiful Jane, chatted with us in front of the house. I asked how it was going with their ecological "touristiculture" and organic production. Oh, it's going quite well, we're almost entirely sustainable, built the guesthouse with driftwood from the beach. I asked her how things had been in Fjöll the other year, when the locals were forced to move away. I don't know, she said; they didn't talk much, those farmers. I asked her to say hello to the brother of the apes.

Found a huge yellowish-white shell on the beach.

B right and early. I'm sitting in the tent opening. The sun shone burning hot through the hole in the sky as I woke. It was a raven that woke me, with a peculiar croaking at three-minute intervals, like the best snooze alarm! I'm grateful to it, because I wouldn't have wanted to miss this sunny moment. Then it changed rhythm, crowed a modern composition followed by shave and a haircut, so long, sucker, and flew off. I was reminded of my deep affection for ravens and their humor, and of the time one helped me herd sheep.

I think they were called the Lamb Mountains that I was supposed to go around, circle counterclockwise and herd back five lambs. I ran, on pins and needles about losing them, had nearly completed my circle and was going to turn back when a raven, sitting on a hill nearby, croaked at me, making the strangest sound I've ever heard from that bird, and letting me know the sheep were right ahead of me. Such great communication that I kept running and found them, and the raven came along to guide me, the blessed bear-berrian, and I followed its advice and herded them back to the farm.

I really wanted to prove myself to something, I don't really know what, maybe to the memory of Grandpa, the farmer, or maybe mostly to the farmer who was with me in the roundup.

You don't really know for whom it is you want to do such a good job. Probably just for life and death.

And then I came here to Vopnafjörður by truck, went to a dance and challenged the alpha hunk to a dance-off and slept on the poet's grave. Well, the ornithologist is stirring in his sleeping bag, having had his slumber. Best to make him some coffee.

Yesterday we filthy pups went to the pool and cleaned ourselves up—we'd been fawned on by a goat yesterday, its smell sweet, but cloying after a while.

We hoped the pool wouldn't be full of tourists, and got our wish; we were alone in the pool and saw merlins playing in the salmon river, were brought coffee as we relaxed in the hot tub.

There's a dense stench of mackerel in the village. The factory purrs here day and night—it's cozy, that sound, said my sweet uncle; it says that there's life in the village. He was so fun last night, played his accordion in a unique, jumpy style that made you wiggle with life and we danced in the living room. Then he showed me pictures of Great-grandma and said that she'd been the funnest person he'd ever known in his life, by far. Fun, how? I asked. Indescribably fun, he said. In these parts, everything's teeming with humor, I feel. But probably some sorrow as well, although its smell is totally different then in the Þingeyjar districts, where the lump in your throat is a deeper blue.

He gave me a register of place names and some other magnificent documents written by himself and others, which he's gathered into two thick portfolios, and told me just to take them; he thought it best that I have them and do with them what I wanted. I didn't know how to take this, whether I should accept them, such trust. So I said I'd make photocopies of the documents in Reykjavík and send them back. I'd better keep my word.

I've taken a peek at these files and they're priceless. Came across an enumeration of the various resources available on "perquisite-farms," for gathering, hunting, collecting, excavating, and utilizing to provide supplemental income: eiderdown, seals, salmon, trout, lumpfish, seabirds and their eggs, copses (for timber), geothermal heat, driftwood, gravel, caves, easy access to the sea for fishing.

We then headed out to Krossavík, where my great-great-grandmother and grandfather lived. A relative of mine met us in front of the house and told us about the place. He comes every year from Germany and stays on the farm with his family. He informed me that our ancestors had been great chieftains. Oh, really? Yes, yes, so they say, bigwigs in this region. What does that mean, actually? Is it a rank given for economic status or poetic style? We weren't sure, but bade him a gracious farewell, and I felt that I liked this new relative of mine, who reminded me of the writer Gunnar Gunnarsson, the two of them being related and having the same delicate-looking lower lip.

We were feeling hungry, so here we sit in a fancy café in the old co-op, where Grandma used to steal raisins, putting them in her little pajama pocket and running up to the toy-attic where her mother kept the French toys she'd ordered from a catalogue: a man who pooped if you gave him a pill and a little toy store with real hard candies and painted cigar boxes; her dad always had cigars for guests. It's cheapest to pay well for quality, he'd said. Yes, and he could allow himself to do so. I asked the woman in charge if she'd heard whether my great-grandfather had been chieftainly or arrogant. No; he'd been a fair man and a good photographer, she said, though perhaps a bit of a dandy.

I think I found the guestroom, where there was a porcelain pitcher in a glass bowl and a decorative towel. Sometimes so many guests that the children had to sleep in a tent in the yard. Laughed themselves senseless as they sang their nonsense verses; sang themselves to sleep: *Too ra loo ra li li, violin, violin, violin* . . .

It's strange to have come to a place I'd heard so much about. I even feel farther from the place now that I'm here inside it than when Grandma described every little nook and cranny, all its patterns and colors, as if she were describing the emotional life within the house at the same time.

I grabbed a booklet about the farms on the heath and sunk myself into a description of how people gave up on the fjord due to a shortage of land—I feel guilty, because I'd just recently read how one of my great-great-ancestors at Bustarfell had appropriated the land there; and what else, yes, how people were forced to move and dug themselves into the sides of hills up on heaths.

On the top floor we met a woman researching this settlement and its history. And another one who has a little research center up in the room where my great-great-grandmother lived, where everyone used to gather around the big stove, and where she could see her old farm through the window. Here they give advice and guidance to the descendants of the Icelandic Canadians who return to their old country and want to visit their family farms. And how do people react? I asked. They all break down crying when they set foot on the land of their ancestors. And the others who might just be tagging along, do they start crying too? Because there's such a peculiarly strong connection to history that seems to move everyone, even when the history isn't their own.

We visited an aunt who always sends Grandma flatbread and jams and good thoughts; she invited us into her beautiful flower conservatory, made of glass, where we could look out over the village and the fjord, and at the flowers, which she grows with great artistry. She's a healer, by the grace of God, and has just learned a new method that I think I need after all my genealogical research: DNA healing.

Last night after we went back to our tent, I kidded around that Birdy needed to bring me down a peg so I wouldn't start thinking of myself as a bigwig! I was slightly worried that he'd fear me growing too domineering, since what stands out in all of these stories about my family is how the women were independent, eccentric, and also domineering, or whatever you call it, bossy . . . . Note to self: be careful of that . . .

She told us about Aunt Salína, who studied woodcarving and forging, carved picture frames and embroidered unique images. Her brother, she said, had an unusually strong sense of preservation, and had wanted the old Bustarfell farmhouse to be maintained and turned into a museum at the same time people were rushing to bulldoze contemptible old farms.

We drove up to Bustarfell. It's really great fun to go there; the old farm gets plenty of air. We glanced at each other when the curator told us the organ had always been played on Sunday mornings. He whispered to me that we should take up that habit in our home, have song time on Sunday mornings. This is how the book of good habits is written.

And there was the little window that my grandmother crawled out of, straight onto the roof, hearing the chickens when she woke and wanting to go to them. It made me think of the papal kitchen in Avignon, the octagonal chimney and the apothecary. And when I came to the boys' loft, I remembered the writings of Guðfinna Þorsteinsdóttir from Teigur, who called herself Erla the Poetess and translated *The Lost Musicians* by William Heinesen. I recall that Guðfinna wrote, among other things, about a man called Jóhann the Nude because he had a great compulsion for exhibitionism, lost his mind, abandoned his farm and roamed around with eighteen bundles hanging from him, filled with treats, medicine, and ink. She also described Jón Eyjólfsson, who was a farmhand at Bustarfell before he too took to the road. Great-grandma had given him an ample portion of sheep's milk gruel, as was customary when the shepherds did a good job, and all the other domestics and farmhands were given extra portions in his honor. Jón didn't want any, but Grandma urged him to take it with him. He put it in his trunk, along with his best brown wool suit. But another farmhand, a foul-tempered, jealous man, snuck up to the loft and shook the trunk, and when Jón opened it, his suit was covered with the slimy stuff. Later, Jón took to the road and was called "Violin," because he learned every song by heart and was asked to sing them at dances. That was before the accordions arrived; he knew all the rhythms, the beatboxer of his time. He was also an unofficial postman and, even though he didn't know how to read, everyone received their letters without fail. He also tried as well as he could to lend a hand to those less fortunate, accepting donations of food and clothing from the wealthier farms and giving them away, like a true Santa Claus.

My aunt from Bustarfell invited us in; she lives next door to the old farm, thus keeping it in our family, as it's been since our ancestress Úlfheiður came out of exile, down from the heath where she'd survived by eating Iceland moss and trout. She showed us a manuscript of the history of Bustarfell, where the same family has been living since the Reformation. I wanted to see it published. And then I asked her about Salína's diary, because the housewife at Refsstaður whispered to me that it existed. It was so dramatic to turn its pages that I felt nearly breathless and couldn't decide what was most important to memorize. It contained all sorts of recipes and fragments of reports. No emotions, except between the lines. Then we took a look at her handiwork. Some of it unfinished. She suffered from something after returning from the West, where she'd gone to fetch her brothers, and contracted typhoid fever and encephalitis. Apparently she wasn't all that good at house-keeping, but was better at other things. Some say she was a lesbian. People say so many things. But a few things we do know. Might she have loved her brother so much that she was incapable of loving others? Birdy asked, looking at me with a smile. In any case, she ended up taking her own life. Around my neck I wear a gold necklace with her name on it. I carve on my shield of hope . . .

We visited Salína's grave on our way back. For a long time it had no gravestone. A shame? We also went to the grave of the Mountain Poet, who died from drinking too much in a small attic-room by the sea. *Darkness descends, the midwinter sun sinks, a cruel-looking gloom-rune on the snowdrift laughs.*

Now we part. And that entire time disappears. Our road lies to the east.

T he first person that I saw when I came inside was my
beloved friend Muggur. Looking very much the old man
in his costume, limping over the river and grimacing, I wanted
to touch the screen and come closer to him, but restrained
myself. No touching.

In *Sons of the Soil*, the movie that the Norwegian or German
woman carried around the country and showed in Quonset
huts and meeting halls, there's this wonderful sentence, as
Muggur looks back sadly at the estate of Borg: *Behind him, the
countryside was peaceful and fair, where life was tranquil, yet filled
with wonderful dreams of the future*. I don't know whether you can
get close to the writer in this place. Before noon, I felt as if I were
managing it, sitting with him for a long time in his office, the
premises enveloped in climbing plants. I browsed through his
books and bumped into these words in *Lament of the Heath*, a
good reminder on a day like this: *The day- and night-currents of
the life that moves restlessly about the estate change only negligibly
with new owners or deaths.*

Then tourists came swarming in from a cruise ship, several
buses, and out front instruments were tuned. Don't you think
we're lucky to have ended up here on the final day of the regional
festival? Sack race and rhubarb fight. The director of the games

shouts into the microphone, and the noise carries in to us. I gnash my teeth in frustration and curse the racket.

I'd imagined sitting here in peace and quiet and connecting myself to the place, trying to understand this longing of Gunnar's to be in charge of an estate. He returned from abroad as a famous writer and settled here, deep in a valley. Perhaps he wanted to prove himself to his farmer father, despite the latter being dead. Or, after turbulent years in Europe, ground himself in the region that fostered him as a boy. Apparently, it took him a long time to find the right farm.

I wanted to walk around the area and find the connection, because at first glance, this isn't the prettiest farmstead; but I'm sure it opens itself up to you after a longer stay. In *Sonata of the Sea*, Gunnar writes: *On a quiet ride through the wide-open habitations and wilderness, a keen observer learns things that cannot be learned in any other way. To those who know how to watch and listen, nature willingly opens all its doors, day and night.*

Yes, it would doubtless be good to stay here for a while. Just remember not to cheat on your wife, remember not to become depressed. They gave up after nine years. Gave the beautiful house to the government, with the stipulation that it be a place for projects on cultural enrichment, a library, a place of healing, an art gallery. And here there's an exhibition about Gunnar and his wife, as well. But how can you really get closer to them?

I was perusing the exhibition on the excavation of the old monastery site. In the gallery, a small boy was also having a look, and when we bumped into each other, we were both equally startled and he was terribly upset at how jumpy he was, absolutely devastated. I said that I was, too, and that we just had to take a deep breath. Yeah, I know, he said. And he added that he tried to ground himself regularly, but often just forgot to. Me too, I said. The concert had started and I gave up on trying to connect to the house, gave in. We went out into the sun and sat up on the hill, had some bread with trout from my grandma in Egilsstaðir, who always prepares such nice picnic lunches. With a malt drink and some heavy rock 'n' roll.

In the area where the ruins of the monastery and the hospital were being excavated, mass was held that afternoon, and the choral group Voces Thules sang old offices, dream verses. It was fun to be able to join in the singing under the open sky.

We rented the old farmhouse at Sléttaleiti in the Suðursveit region for a few days. Divided the space between us, and luckily both of us liked better what the other disliked. So I'm upstairs, with a view of the hillside, and he's downstairs facing the sea. I usually like looking at the sea, but there's a road here between it and us, and I seem to have more difficulty ignoring the traffic than he does.

I wrote up a schedule to make things easier for us here. When we'll wake up, when we'll eat and have coffee, when we'll take walks and go fishing, and when we'll have sex and sleep. It's proven good for us these three days; we vary the plan and enjoy screwing it up completely and turning it upside down, but the division of the day is what counts. To split up the space correctly and divide the time right. That's the main thing. But it can never be done, once and for all. There has to be some flexibility within each timeframe to discuss the plan and listen to different points of view, and within the shared space there has to be a place for such discussions. And to change one's mind.

I've really liked waking up at the crack of dawn lately. But now I find that I'm more like Sesam in *Sonata of the Sea*, who cherished "næturnæði"—the quiet of the night. I didn't even know that this word existed. *Næturnæði*.

We went to Bjöllugil Ravine yesterday. The car did well, joggling over the roaring glacier rivers. We got stuck at the top, couldn't get back because of the landslides, and had to take a narrow path so close to the edge of the ravine that I felt dizzy. We'd accidentally followed a sheep track rather than a human one. On our way back down we filled our pockets and bags with birch and willow leaves that we'd gathered. Birdy quoted Þórbergur regularly, having just read his book about this area and its people, describing every little patch with great artistry.

It was in this ravine that the Irish monks called *papar* supposedly threw their bells as they fled from the Norse settlers. I'm feeling fairly excited again about these *papar* stories, and now my Owlie is documenting every cave in the South. But the catch is that there's very little or no evidence of the *papar* settlement, because it's literally pre-historic, as is the entire settlement of Iceland, in fact. I'm wondering what sort of views they held of the land. Maybe they, both men and women, hadn't given a thought to claiming land, owning land, settling a land. And in that sense, they can't be counted as settlers—neither frontiersmen nor -women.

It's nice to be in this house. The writer Einar Bragi, who spent summers here as a boy, donated it to the Icelandic Writers' Union. But I'm not sure that much land comes with it. At least not much independence. Because there's nowhere to throw out your garbage. Maybe garbage is a problem everywhere in Iceland. It must bode ill not to pay as much attention to your waste as to your progress.

I'd planned to dive into writing, but got stuck reading some old editions of the journal *Birtingur* and articles by Einar Bragi.

And I've also been comparing different versions of his poems. He emended and republished them, and instructed his readers to burn the earlier versions. I got chills when I read that; felt that I really understood where he was coming from. The regret. Or the compulsion to emend. And he's absolutely right—the poems just get better and better. On the other hand, it's impossible to destroy older versions; it's fun to read them all together.

Well, according to schedule, I'm going to cook a tiny fillet of char that my dear Birdy just caught. Then take a walk alongside the mountain, write for two hours and cuddle up for the night.

Of course, you certainly don't need to own the land you inhabit. There are so many beautiful houses all over the country and the world that you can stay in for little expense. But by the power of my rights as a member of the Writers' Union, I recommend that something be done about the garbage. Make sure the cycle is in order. Shouldn't circular thinking be ingrained in islanders?

The char was so freshly caught and freshly dead that it twitched in the frying pan. Death spasms for dinner.

There was a news story about the discovery of an old road that the soldiers of Boudica, the queen of the Druids, had used in their struggle against Roman rule. I'm relieved to know that they're still looking for roads that lead somewhere besides outrageous expansion.

We rambled down to the Þórbergur museum this morning. I was surprised to see so few of the writer's books on the shelves in the lobby, which were mostly drowning in tourist crap: puffin pillows and buffs. Where's the spirit of the writer? *Take from me, God, all sauce swill*, muttered Birdy. We wondered if the tourist shop would be better off in a little hut next to the museum. So that you could walk into the world of Þórbergur, instead of into the world of Icelandic desperation over tourists not buying enough. I know this sounds stupid and arrogant, because what do I know about running a business? But couldn't the writer be a bit more visible?

On the other hand, this thing with the houses of writers and artists is fairly mind-boggling. Strange phenomenon. Is it a given that only the houses of males are opened as museums, or what? At the moment, I can't remember a single woman's home that was turned into a museum. Well, the Gerður Museum is named after a woman, but it wasn't her home. Maybe it would be anachronistic to establish museums for them now. More appropriate to dedicate open space to them, perhaps? You should open a museum, said my little nephew when he walked into my chaos. All homes are, in some sense, museums. People surround themselves with things that remind them of the lives they once longed to live.

I recall the museum homes: Hnitbjörg, the house of Einar Jónsson (he and his wife slept in separate beds; his wife had no space to call her own—only he did); Ásmundur's domed house and the Ásmundur Gallery both having been his homes, with enough space for everyone; Halldór Laxness's house, Gljúfrasteinn, with its salon living room; Skriðuklaustur and the Sigurjón Museum, as well as the reconstruction of Þórbergur's house at his birthplace. I can't recall other houses at the moment. Except, yes, Bulgakov's apartment in Kiev, which is a memorable museum, so memorable that I hardly have any recollection of it. But there was a certain spirit in the things there, between them. On his spot.

The other day I dreamed of the red jasper that's used in printing, and then I saw a picture of it in an exhibition about the convent that was located here. Tonight I dreamed of calligraphy, a woman with her hand in a sling and her head wrapped in leaves. Stood today on the convent doorstep and gazed at the sea. Apparently there were a number of buildings clustered together: each and every nun had her own prayer cell, and they would meet in the convent garden and the weaving room. The nuns made their living by weaving. When I thought about their weaving, I felt as if I better understood the slogan "work and pray." That it really had to do with love. Living in this convent for a period of time was an Abbess Oddný, my namesake, the sister of the chieftain Gissur the White. The two of them were close. Like Oswald and Ebba in Northumbria, and in both cases, the siblings worked hard together to cultivate the devotional life. Question of whether this sibling bond is an alternative to brotherhood. Is exclusivity fundamental to siblinghood, as it is to brotherhood? Maybe the leaf-adorned stone is a mark of a love between siblings that is all-embracing yet never exclusive or secretive.

Together, we went to a kind of open-air church-floor. We didn't get engaged, but almost; the atmosphere was rather dramatic. On hexagonal basalt, eroded by the sea and forming a stage in the middle of a pasture. We met the priest on the way back and he told us, out of the blue, that the Celts had held their masses out in the open and that marriage had an entirely different meaning in that tradition. I ran after him and wanted to hear more, whether it might have been a kind of side-tradition that hardly exists except in the subconscious. But he was in a hurry; had to say mass in three places before midnight.

Yesterday evening there was a regional festival and me and Birdy, my feathered suitor, tried to go to every event, to support local culture and be good sports. Everyone did such a great job; the organist was kept very busy, the church choir sang, and there were films and concerts. Birdy asked me if I felt we'd made a good showing at this festival, but I said we still needed to visit the museum and the crafts market. There I heard someone talking about trash-burning and the pollution it causes. District politics and pollution. Then a local told me that the nuns had run to meet the monks, who lived in Álftaver; they'd paired up like fulmars in small caves in the black cliffs and cackled late into the night.

I'm trying to calm myself down and take a deep breath. But I've got tears in my eyes and a lump in my throat. We were watching the news and the first story was that Hólsfjöll had been sold. I couldn't believe my ears. I called home and spoke to Dad and Mom; they were upset but said that luckily, it hadn't actually been sold yet. Although a binding contract had been signed, it was illegal to sell such a large tract of land to a foreign buyer.

My father's brothers, foster brothers, probably feel that it's their own private business if they choose to sell the land that my grandfather left to them in the belief that they would continue to farm it.

In the news report, a spokesman said that this was an enormously positive investment that would bring in other investors—implying that the North was now safe. He also stated that the Chinese businessman wasn't thinking about profit; he was a romantic idealist and conservationist. They really know how to present themselves. I've heard this all before, dear. I haven't studied the evolution of the modern colonial lords for nothing. And did someone ask to have a look at the contract? Does it contain any stipulations about conservation? Who exactly are the intermediaries in this case? It wouldn't surprise me if it were all filthy with corruption, like so many times before when a good business deal is supposedly made on behalf of the public. The worst thing is that some people actually believe that it will provide them with a few breadcrumbs. But it should be remembered that we're not a starving nation. *May he who refuses to save you be repaid with fire*, one might easily have said on such an occasion. And what would Snoop Dogg have said? *Raise your motherfucking hands to the sky?*

And Stjáni, our Mountain-Poet Kristján, what would he have said?

> *All alone in cold of night*
> *Over desolate sands I roam.*
> *Now the North is gone from my sight,*
> *Now I have no home.*

I'm in a timber hut, with a view of the lake and Skjaldbreiður. Eyowl invited me to stay at her place here, and then, after informing me last night that she had to leave, asked if I wanted to stay, if I were in need of quietude.

Among other things, we talked about how much had been accomplished in Iceland since the economic collapse. The soil was more fertile, and was covered with beautiful sprouts. But they'll need further nurturing. And you've got to nurture your family, she said. My own little family? It's good to be reminded every now and then that my biological clock is ticking. And there I see the moon, it just came out from under that cloud, reddish-yellow and nearly full.

I'm not at all afraid here. The warmth of friendship fills the place. Books and music and seven ravens that let you know if danger is approaching. And a stuffed owl that knows how things stand.

I drink green tea and eat purple seaweed and almonds.

Birdy is coming to get me tomorrow. I miss him. Yet it's good to be alone, think, and note the position of the sun, as Mom says.

I went outside earlier and picked a boxful of brambleberries and blueberries. To sit alone like that and eat blueberries with cream and think about existence, gaze at the lake; it's not such a bad place to be in life. Grandma called me the day before yesterday and asked if I could be a dear and pop over to the store for her and buy some blueberries and maybe a spot of cream; she suddenly had a huge craving. And also to see me. It was a very unusual call. I went to her, and found out she was dying.

I aired out her comforter. Tried to do what Mom does when I'm ill; come with a moist cloth and lay it on my forehead and wash my face, readjust the pillows.

I'm not exactly sad, but I feel her loss deeply. Now the funnest person in the world is simply gone.

On the memorial, beneath the bust of the poet she was so fond of, is a line from a poem: *If you come across my mother, whisper her my regards, wherever she might be.*

Yes, I'll do that, dearest, happily. And might I ask you, if you come across my little grandmother in her white beret and she doesn't know where she's going, to please show her the way home? But where was her home? Where did she live on this earth? Where did she spend most of her time? I never asked her.

There's a trampoline next to the house here, and before the sun said its goodbyes I took my shoes off and jumped, looking at the islands. It's a bit odd, jumping alone. For such a long time. I thought that if I had little ones, I would always be telling them to watch out for the metal poles. I wondered if it was possible to plant some cushion pink or moss all around the mat; it's a pity how badly moss takes being replanted. And when I imagined that I was hopping in moss, I remembered my grandma telling me how she and her sisters used to jump around in the mounds of wool in the fall, and roll around in the snow at Christmas, and I started crying. Strange thing, jumping and crying at the same time.

I thought about how, if the Almighty and nature allow me to have children, it's too late for me to introduce them to Grandma and hear her recite poems to them. But I shook it off, jumped a bit more and decided to try to learn those poems. Try to communicate her joy to them, if they're ever born. Grant them a share in all the beautiful memories.

GRAVE MOUND,
BELLMAS UNDER OPEN SKY

On our pilgrimage around the country, long before we arrived in the fearsomely beautiful fjord Berufjörður, I saw a memorial to the poet Kristján at Djúpilækur. The inscription stated that Kristján's Lord's Prayer consisted of the words *beauty, joy, tranquility*. I've noticed that a lot of good phenomena have "y's" in them. And *it would be nice to know what dwells in the water's mind*.

Owlie has opened the grave mound. First he found beautiful beads strung on an ancient umbilical cord. Then he came across a woman—an old woman with worn wisdom teeth and wrecked knees. Likely from around the year 700. What? Well, that's what the tephra layer indicates. Ash from the year 730 settled over the grave. And then a little bell came to light—or, not exactly "to light," because it's still all covered in dirt; it can't be cleaned off right away. The artifact specialist believes it to be a home bell. To call the household to prayer.

We're staying in a tent next to it, Birdy and I. The tent is like an upside-down ivy leaf, did you notice? he asked. I lie inside it and daydream about the opening of the mound. What more will be revealed, and what will it mean? This is so exciting that I'm about to burst. Pagan graves and grave goods, pagan graves and grave goods.

They went for a walk along the hillside above us, but I'm going to take a little slumber, half-awake, half-asleep. Below me, down in the ground, are forms that haunt my mind. Dark green pentagons. Copper-colored octagons. Deep blue squares. A farm created from many forms. I catch a whiff of medicinal herbs from the columns of steam in the democracy farm; no, I'm not talking about the commonwealth farm, but the democracy farm. Even though I don't know where that farm should be, I know that I'll have peace and quiet there. If it's not too late. Fucking exterminationists. No, don't blame others. And don't forget, either. Don't smooth over. Allow justice to arise from the earth. My dreams have disoriented me. I think I'll crawl out of the tent, go to the grave mound and look inside. Maybe I can lie down there for a few moments and see whether I dream something amazing. Beyond my grave, gaping, cold. In mold our honor lies.

GRAVE MOUND,
MIGRANT BIRD DAY,
V-FORMATION DAY AND FEAST OF ST. FRANCIS,
WHO UNDERSTOOD BIRD LANGUAGE

I must have fallen asleep in the grave, and some dirt crumbled onto me. I woke up feeling like I was suffocating. But they hurried to me, the ornithologists and archaeologists. Dug me up like a dead old woman. It took me a moment to get my bearings, rocking back and forth. Felt as if Georges Bataille and Michel Leiris were there beside me, heard them speaking French and tried to answer them—*oui oui*. Then heard Leiris say, sagely: *Et j'ai choisi, pour le signe sous lequel les placer le nom tout à la fois floral et souterrain de Perséphone, arraché ainsi à ses noirceurs terrestres et haussé jusqu'au ciel d'une tête de chapitre . . .*

I cleared the dirt from my nose and mouth and sat in the ornithologist's lap as they designed the future. They said that we should build ourselves a farm like the ones from the fourteenth century, in the wilderness, with a steam bath and printing press, where seasonal memories will be printed and almanacs reborn, as well. They said that we should live with our families and good friends in a sustainable, permacultural manner, using the latest technology, in deep-rooted friendship, and connected to the earth yet with our doors open to the sea.

Our extended family might have to live in the wilderness sometimes, sometimes in a cave or up in a tree, out on an island or down at the coast, all depending on how our natural cycles connect us to the sea and the land, heaven and hell, I said. Would that be possible? Yes, of course, it will certainly be possible to move from place to place, change things up, they said.

We could start by building ourselves a birdhouse, with this old prayer hovering above its entrance: *May your troubles be less and your blessings be more, and nothing but happiness come through your door.*

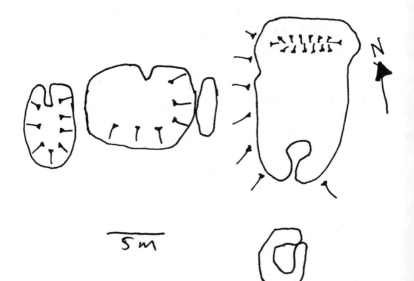

Plan of ruins

GLOSSARY

Festivals and Holidays in Land of Love and Ruins

BURSTING DAY (Ice. *Sprengidagur*): Shrove Tuesday, when Icelanders traditionally eat salted lamb and split pea soup.

FIRST DAY OF SUMMER (Ice. *sumardagurinn fyrsti*): An annual public holiday in Iceland, held on the first Thursday after April 18. Traditionally, this was a rather important holiday, when people would exchange gifts and hold dinner parties, but it is much less festive now (apart from public celebrations, including parades, etc.).

FEAST OF THE CROSS (Ice. *krossmessa á vori*): May 3; commemorates the discovery of the True Cross of Christ in Jerusalem in 326, by Saint Helena (c. 252– c. 330), the mother of the Roman emperor Constantine the Great (c. 272–337). For Icelanders, it is a "moving day," when farmhands and domestic workers change households and employers.

RENT DAY (Ice. *eldaskildagi*): May 10; traditionally, the day when sheep that crofters raised for landowners and priests during the winter were returned to their owners, and when other types of rents were collected.

ICELANDIC REPUBLIC DAY: (Ice. *lýðveldisdagurinn* and also called *Þjóðhátíðardagurinn*, or "The National Holiday") June 17; commemorates the founding of the Icelandic Republic (and independence from Denmark) on that day in 1944.

FEAST OF THE BEHEADING: August 29; commemorates the martyrdom of John the Baptist by beheading on the orders of Herod Antipas, at the request of his stepdaughter Salome and her mother.

FEAST OF ST. GALL: October 16; according to legend, the Irish missionary St. Gall (c. 550–c. 646) was followed around by a bear that had charged him and been rebuked by him one night in the woods in what is now Switzerland.

WINTER FEAST OF ST. ÞORLÁKUR: December 23; Þorlákur Þórhallsson (1133–1193) was bishop of the see of Skálholt in southern Iceland and is Iceland's patron saint (officially recognized as a saint by the Catholic Church in 1984).

ÞORRI: The name for the fourth winter month according to the old Icelandic calendar, from mid-January to mid-February.

MAN-OF-THE-HOUSE DAY (Ice. *bóndadagur*): the first day of the month of Þorri. On this day, the man of the house was traditionally supposed to welcome in the month by running around the outside of the house wearing just a shirt and one leg of his long underwear, dragging the other leg behind him. Nowadays on *bóndadagur*, the "lady of the house" is supposed to treat her male partner exceptionally well with gift-giving and the like.

WINTERTIME DAY OF PRAYER (Ice. *Bænadagur að vetri*): In Iceland, the fourth Sunday after Epiphany (late January), when the gospel story of how Jesus stilled the sea and wind is read in church (Matthew 8:23–7), and prayers are made particularly for fishermen, before the start of the winter fishing season on February 3.

FEAST OF THE VISITATION: July 2 (though moved to May 31 in the papal revision of the liturgical year in 1969); the feast commemorates the visit of Mary, pregnant with Jesus, to her cousin Elizabeth, who was pregnant with John the Baptist. According to the Biblical account of this visitation (in Luke), John, recognizing the divinity of Jesus, leapt for joy in Elizabeth's womb, at which point Elizabeth declared Mary blessed, and Mary responded with the Magnificat ("My soul doth magnify the Lord"), a canticle that is reserved for this feast day.

MIDSUMMER DAY (Ice. *Jónsmessa*): June 24; also St. John's Day (Feast of the Nativity of St. John the Baptist).

WOMAN-OF-THE-HOUSE DAY (Ice. *konudagur*): Like *bóndadagur* (Man-of-the-House Day), but when women are treated especially well by their husbands or boyfriends. This day, always a Sunday, marks the start of the month of Góa, the fifth month in the old Icelandic calendar (the eighteenth week of winter, or what corresponds to mid-February to mid-March).

SKERPLA: The name of the eighth month according to the old Icelandic calendar, starting around May 21.

SUMMER FEAST OF ST. ÞORLÁKUR: July 20; commemorates the translation of his relics on that day in 1198 (see above for St. Þorlákur).

FEAST OF ST. FRANCIS: October 4. The Italian St. Francis of Assisi (1181/82–1226) is said to have had a great love for all animals, and particularly birds.

ODDNÝ EIR ÆVARSDÓTTIR was born in 1972. She completed a doctoral minor degree at Paris-Sorbonne University, as well as carrying out research in Icelandic museum field studies. She has written three autobiographical novels, translated and edited literary works, organized visual arts events, and ran a visual arts space in New York and Reykjavík (Dandruff Space) in collaboration with her brother, archaeologist Uggi Ævarsson. Together they run the publishing company Apaflasa (Monkey Dandruff). She has also worked as editor of the environmental web site Náttúra.info. *Heim til míns hjarta* was nominated for the cultural prize of the newspaper *DV* in 2009. *Land of Love and Ruins (Jarðnæði)* was nominated for the Icelandic Literary Award in 2011 and won the Icelandic Women's Literature Prize in 2012.

ABOUT THE TRANSLATOR

PHILIP ROUGHTON is an award-winning translator of Icelandic literature. He earned a PhD in Comparative Literature from the University of Colorado, Boulder, with specialties in medieval Icelandic, medieval Chinese, and Latin literature, and wrote his dissertation on medieval Icelandic translations of saints' and apostles' lives. He has taught modern and world literature at CU-Boulder, and medieval literature at the University of Iceland. His translations include works by many of Iceland's best-known writers, including the Nobel laureate Halldór Laxness, Jón Kalman Stefánsson, Bergsveinn Birgisson, Steinunn Sigurðardóttir, and others. He was awarded the 2015 American-Scandinavian Foundation Translation Competition Prize for his translation of Halldór Laxness' novel *Gerpla* (*Wayward Heroes*), the 2016 Oxford-Weidenfeld Prize for his translation of Jón Kalman Stefánsson's *The Heart of Man*, and an NEA Literature Translation Fellowship for 2017.